MURDER AT SEA

Ankit Jajoo

For my grandfather, who introduced me to the world of mystery.

1

Ash needed a vacation. For months, he had been surrounded by depressed, anxious, obsessive patients, and that takes a toll eventually. He was sitting in his office, just finished up with the day's work when Hemant walks in with a dumbbell in each hand.

"1, 2, 1, 2...Hey, how's everything going, Ash?" Hemant said without panting once.

"Nothing much, just chilling, kinda tired though," Ash sighed.

Hemant puts down the dumbbells and starts doing pushups on the floor of the office. "I'm going on this cruise, super exclusive, just a handful of high-end people to Fiji, so I'm trying to get a beach bod by then," Hemant mentions while starting to do lunges.

"Yo, that sounds like so much fun, wish I could go, I seriously need a vacation," said Ash.

Hemant jumps up and exclaims, "Wait, no way! You are in luck, I got an extra ticket from my clients if you want to join." Hemant was an accomplished accountant raking in eight figures a year from high profile clients. Of course, nobody actually understood how Hemant became so popular of an accountant, Ash didn't even know he could actually leave the

1

gym for long enough to run a couple numbers.

Ash couldn't believe it, a real cruise, a real vacation, no worries about what is bothering a client, just a beach, water, free food all around. He couldn't let this opportunity go to waste and said, "I would love to go. That would be awesome, I'm so down."

Hemant throws the ticket over and said, "See you in two days at the San Francisco port." He picks up the dumbbells and starts to leave.

"Take it easy, take it easy," Ash replied.

***

Ron drained a 3 — his tenth of the night in less than two minutes. He decided to take a break and check his phone. This was a first for him, he used to never carry his phone anywhere, but then his boss yelled at him and almost fired him for never responding to urgent messages. His boss sent a message: "Ron, you're needed on this ship. There is a huge businessman named Jason Spark, we need to sign an agreement with him and I'm giving you this responsibility. If you don't succeed, don't even bother coming back from the cruise; there is no use for you anymore. Your tickets are attached, its the USS Carr, and leaves from the San Francisco port in 48 hours and goes to Fiji. Go home and get packing, I know you're in the gym shooting 3s as usual."

Ron was used to this behavior, he was threatened to be fired more often than Steph shooting a 3. He looked at the ticket and immediately became intrigued. Not everyone gets to go to Fiji on a high end cruise every weekend. Why him? He just started at this company a few years ago and he didn't have a very high ranking job. His boss also didn't even like him. And Jason Spark? He's a whale that the entire world was trying to capture. He was literally the Moby Dick of every single business in the world, a reclusive billionaire who no one ever sees who has so much money sitting in the bank account that it makes even banks look cheap. If he was a country, he would be one of the top 20 richest countries in the world. But the boss' word is law.

"Fiji, huh?" Ron thought while making another 3.

***

Danny was busy on his computer coding when the email flashed. He always used to code in his free time, it was his hobby, his job, his life, everything. He was the typical person who would sit in their mom's basement for years in a dark room coding. And he was. Despite his best efforts, he couldn't hold on to a job for too long and couldn't afford rent anywhere in the city. It didn't help that he lived in San Francisco either.

Danny clicked on the email, which did a little dance on his screen. It read, "You are invited! Congratulations, congratulations, congratulations!!! For an all inclusive cruise to Fiji on the well-named USS Carr! Sand…beaches…a vacation of a lifetime, all yours if you just click this link to confirm your reservation! What can possibly be better? Oh, I know, it's COMPLETELY FREE! That's right, not a single dime, penny, nickel, or Benjamin. Confirm now for a trip you'll remember forever!" Danny was rightfully suspicious. *There's no way this is real. This is about as real as a Nigerian prince who needs money,* Danny thought while about to click delete when his phone rang.

"Hello?" Danny asked. A cheery voice responded, "Hi, this is Amanda from Carr Reservations. I just wanted to check in with you to confirm if you would be joining us on our maiden voyage to Fiji." Danny was so confused and was trying to understand why someone would play such an elaborate prank on him, but he went with it. "Why, yes, I'm free and would love to join," Danny replied. "Awesome, I'll have the ticket sent right over. Have a great night," Amanda said and disconnected. Lo and behold, two minutes later, another email flashed with a cruise ticket. Danny looked carefully at it. It was somehow actually real? Danny couldn't believe his eyes, why would someone send him a ticket to a cruise to Fiji?

He was a nobody. So he started wondering to himself, maybe it was the competition he won, but no that was just a small hackathon, how how could that be? Then he started wondering maybe he had some friends in high places, but then he realized he doesn't have any friends, not anymore. Then he decided he might as well go to the cruise and find out why he got these tickets and hope that it wasn't just some sort of elaborate scam. He began packing.

***

Samantha emerged from the pool. This was her normal routine, every night swimming for one kilometer as exercise and really a stress-reliever. However, on this particular instance, she was interrupted about 850 meters in due to her phone ringing and was incredibly upset. *This better be good,* she grumbled to herself. She walked over to her phone and picked it up. It was her boss. *Ugh, what does he want now?,* thought Samantha.

"Samantha, I got a job for you. You have to fly to San Francisco where there is this cruise ship on its way to Fiji, the USS Carr. It's only the top 1% of the 1% allowed on that ship, which is why you got to go. Imagine all the photo opportunities of all the top people in the world you can get. Also, rumor has it that the elusive billionaire Jason Spark will be on board. Nobody's ever gotten a picture of him in over 10 years, you got to be the one. You'll make our newspaper famous. No ifs or buts, you are going. I already booked your flight tickets and the cruise ticket, your flight leaves in two hours, get ready now and go!" Her boss rattled off and then hung up as if he was still on a pay as you go plan and was about to pay another cent to talk.

Wow, no hello Samantha or sorry for disturbing you Samantha or even, God-forbid, asking me if I actually could do this job, Samantha thought to herself. Cursing to herself, she started packing. As she was packing, she started thinking again, this isn't really that bad. Jason Spark was one of the biggest names in photography, and if she got his picture, she would be world famous. Oh she need to go shopping. How could she ever mingle with the rest of the crowd in ratted jeans and a T-shirt? She hoped that this was covered by the company. Time to get started, she thought.

***

Aron was walking around in his Oxford T-shirt after his photo shoot. Now, Aron didn't go to Oxford. In fact, he had absolutely no connection to Oxford other than he liked the name. But that didn't stop him before, nor will it stop him now. His wardrobe looked like the USNews top 100 colleges world rankings. There were the staple Ivy leagues such as Harvard, Yale, Princeton. The engineering schools such as MIT or Caltech. Even a couple state schools with UVA, Berkeley, and Michigan making appearances. The one school he didn't have nor will ever have is UNC. He had a reputation to uphold, choosing the right blue and going to Duke.

Aron was a man on a mission, this particular day, however. He walked up to his photography boss and stormed into the office. "I heard there was this ship, the USS Carr, that was on its maiden voyage to Fiji and all the big names of the world, including Jason Spark are going to be onboard. I also heard Samantha was going to take pictures of them and she'll become famous. I can't stand that, you know that. You have to send me onto that ship, too. Our newspaper will be the famous one with me being the better photographer," Aron ranted.

His boss looked at him over his glasses and said, "Sure. I

was going to send you anyway."

Aron was taken aback. He had practiced a whole argument to convince his boss to let him go; he did not think that his boss would be that ready to let him go. For once, he was speechless. "I'll send your tickets within the hour. Go along now," his boss dismissed him.

Yes! I got the job. Now, I'll show Samantha. Since our Duke days, we've been competing and I can't back down now. I will be the better photographer and be more famous than she ever will be. Jason Spark is mine, Aron thought to himself as he started to walk home to plan which colleges he should take to represent on the ship.

***

Aldrich was playing golf. This was his typical pastime since he had no substantial endeavor to complete anymore. He had manufactured billions from an "import/export business." No one actually knew what he did, just that he wasn't just prosperous or wealthy, he was excessively affluent, much to the ire of everyone around him. He hit the golf ball. "Great shot," exclaimed his servant, Alfred. Aldrich had hit the ball six inches with the hole being 100 feet away, but that didn't stop the paid compliments.

Another servant came running to Aldrich bearing mail. Aldrich stopped his game and received the envelope from the servant. It was engraved in fancy letters saying "To Aldrich." Aldrich wasn't impressed. "What is this engraving? It is too insipid, has no elegance or flair. It isn't even worth my time to pause my excellent game to open this envelope. Here, Alfred, you open it," Aldrich ranted and went back to his game. Alfred opened the envelope and began reading, "To Aldrich, You have been invited to a once in a lifetime opportunity aboard the USS Carr on its maiden voyage to Fiji." Below that, there was a personal note saying: "Dear friend, for old times sake, please come on this voyage. I would really love to have you by my side as we take on the world again, just like we did all those years ago. Your friend, Jason Spark." Aldrich stopped immediately, spun around, and marched to Alfred and snatched the letter. He then ripped up the letter and threw it all over the ground and stormed off back into the mansion. He was going to go look for a matchbox. He was going to burn this letter so that every single memory of Jason was gone. Alfred hurried after him. The last time Aldrich got into this mood, he burnt down one of his guest houses. They ended up losing $50 million in real estate value. Alfred sincerely hoped that Aldrich wouldn't do something so drastic again, but who knows? It's Aldrich after all.

Aldrich was muttering to himself, "the nerve…who does he think he is, asking me, Aldrich Appleton, to join him on this cruise…I can't believe it, he's unbelievable…ugh." Aldrich then straightened up, as if a lightbulb flashed over his head and began maniacally, "Alfred, I will travel on this voyage and I will give Jason Spark what's coming to him or my name isn't Aldrich Appleton!"

2

James Smith wandered down the port, looking for his friend Quentin Vance. James couldn't understand how he lost Quentin. After all, Quentin sticks out like a sore thumb. *Sore thumb is such a weird expression*, James thought. *I mean, how often do people really have sore thumbs and even if they do, does it really stick out? Why not a sore pinkie or sore big toe? The English language just doesn't make sense, and British English is even worse, like why have a "u" in color or gray with an "e?" What even is a lorry or reckon? That's it, I really have to stop spending so much time with Quentin. He and his upper-class British tendencies are really getting me. Where did he even go? How hard can it be to find the one British man who has a monocle as if he was born in 1934 and has electric blue hair like a rockstar? Of course, with his luck, every single person on the dock would have monocles or would be British or would have electric blue hair or all three.*

James was prone to such discussions in his head, which really only started after he met Quentin. He continued to wander around when somebody tapped him on the shoulder. Surprised, James turned around, looking for electric blue hair or a monocle. Instead, he saw nobody. He then looks down and sees a woman. Now James was not a tall man, of average height around 5'9" so it surprised him when he was over a head taller than her. "Hi, I'm Samantha. I was just trying to find this ship, the USS Carr that's going to Fiji. Could you help me?" She queried.

"Sure, I was going down the exact same way, I'm trying to find my friend Quentin, you don't happen to have seen him, have you? He's about your height, electric blue hair with a monocle," James replied.

"Sorry, I haven't. Although if I do see him, I will definitely notice him now. Electric blue hair? That's shocking," Samantha said while laughing at her own pun. James sighed, he hated puns. Wordplay just wasn't funny to him. And this wasn't even a good pun. Actually, on further reflection, he realized he hated other people's puns. He loved his own puns, no matter how poor other people found them. He continued to wander around with Samantha in tow, trying to find the elusive USS Carr and Quentin.

***

Two hours of wordplay from Samantha later, right before boarding, James found Quentin. Quentin, as usual, was in a crowd of women, all of whom were a great deal taller than him.

"Hey Quentin, we got to go like now. Where were you?" James yelled.

Quentin shot the women an apologetic smile and started walking to James and Samantha. "Hey, sorry I'm late. Got caught up. And who is this beautiful lady?" Quentin inquired.

"Stop trying. You're not James Bond, you're a short guy with blue hair," James retorted.

Quentin ignored him. "Let me guess, you're a photographer who is here to go on the trip to Fiji that is leaving in 27 minutes that we are all late to. You are definitely employed by either a member of the ship to take photographs or some external company intended to take photographs of some of the people on board, perhaps even Jason Spark. You are originally from Arizona and attended Duke University. You have just flown in three hours ago, but have been searching for the ship for the past two hours. Photography, though, is just a part time job for you. You intend to become a doctor, eventually, but have taken photography as a way to pay for medical school, even though you like photography a great deal and are considerably good at it. You were recently engaged, but that engagement has since been broken off, probably by someone else, not you or your ex-fiance. His name begins with an A, possibly. You are yet to move on, even though you're actively trying to. Am I right? What's my score?" Quentin said without losing a beat.

Samantha was stunned. "That's completely right. There's no way. Have we met before?" Samantha said after regaining her thoughts.

No way, she couldn't say anything? She has been talking nonstop for the past two hours and one thing from Quentin and speechless? How? James wondered.

"Nope, there's just many things about you that stick out," Quentin replied. *Here he goes again*, thought James. "You're definitely a photographer because I can see a camera lens sticking out of your backpack. That particular lens is extremely expensive, which makes me think that you are probably a professional photographer or you wouldn't be buying that lens if it's just a hobby. Of course, you could be incredibly rich, but even the incredibly rich don't just buy expensive camera lenses for free, considering the bag it's in is considerably less expensive. Now, you are with James, which leads me to believe that you must be going on the same ship or why would you be accompanying James. Sorry, old friend, but you're not really one who attracts anybody, not on this dock. This ship was advertised for the highly exclusive elite, it was a marvel I even have tickets. So considering you're not incredibly rich or you wouldn't really be traveling with that bag, you probably weren't invited on the ship, but rather came because of work.

"Since you are a photographer, you were either hired by a person on the ship or a company trying to obtain photos on someone on the ship, the latter being more likely. There's only one person on the ship who is worth taking pictures of, and that is Jason Spark, who we all know but have never seen. Your baggage tag on your backpack that you failed to remove indicates a flight from Arizona that should have arrived three hours ago. The port is only one hour away from the airport, suggesting that you have been wandering for the past two hours, trying to find the ship itself with James, since I also 'lost' James about two hours ago. However, your watch indicates eastern time zone because you have forgotten to change it to California time yet, meaning you probably work or study somewhere on the east coast. In your front pocket, you can see the semblance of a Duke ID, and a medical one at that, meaning you are studying medicine at Duke University. Since you are studying medicine, you obviously must be taking photography as a part time job, not a hobby, or you wouldn't be all the way out here. Plus hobbyist photographers don't really care for Jason Spark, they care for scenery and nature and maybe various aspects of cities, all of which you can get without traveling over the entire country. The only reason people take part time jobs as a medical student would be to pay for medical school, you wouldn't have time otherwise as part of residency or you would be making enough money as a full-fledged doctor.

"Finally, the part about the engagement. Your finger shows a ring tan, which suggests you were recently engaged, but now the ring is gone, which means the engagement has been broken off and you are trying to move on. However, your heart pendant around your neck was probably a gift from your ex-fiance and is engraved with both of your initials, A and S, which means his name probably started with an A. You obviously still wear the pendant, so you still aren't over him because it has sentimental value, which comes to my final point about someone else breaking off the engagement. If it was you, you wouldn't have trouble removing the pendant and getting over him, and if it was him, you would be so angry, you wouldn't hold on to his gift. This leaves one final explanation that a third person broke it off. Of course, this is all probability. There was never a guarantee any of this was true, just that it was likely," Quentin said in rapid-fire.

Samantha's jaw dropped. "You're...you're... like Sherlock Holmes," she stammered out.

"Bah, Sherlock Holmes is fiction. I mean, looking at cigar smoke, come on, Doyle thinks we're all fools. Sherlock Holmes is an insult to real detectives," he said. *Of course, he's going on about how he's better than Sherlock Holmes, again. He never stops, does he?* James thought.

"I am Quentin Vance, the world's greatest detective, at your service, my lady," Quentin announced.

***

An hour later, they went through security and were all on the ship and went to their respective rooms, deciding to meet up for dinner. James walked into his room and his jaw dropped. It was beautiful. Everything was golden. The bed was a decorated king size bed complete with exquisite pillows and blankets. There was a balcony opening up to a private hot tub and a wonderful view of the ocean. To his left there was another balcony overlooking the main promenade and dining hall. James was in paradise. He decided to take a quick nap before he explored the rest of the ship.

Two hours later, he goes down to meet with Samantha and Quentin for dinner dressed in his nicest tuxedo. He found

Samantha and Quentin sitting on a table with another man he hadn't met before. This man looked deep in thought and was carefully surveying the rest of the room.

"James, how nice of you to join us. I was just talking to Samantha to get to know more about her," Quentin said.

"Oh come on. You know basically everything about me as it is. You're so intelligent and observant, it's amazing," Samantha replied.

"You flatter me. Anyway, James, meet Ash. Ash is a psychiatrist, he came here with his friend Hemant, who is currently trying to find the gym. He's a really interesting guy," Quentin introduced.

"Hey, what's good? James, right? It's really nice to meet you," Ash said.

"Nice to meet you, too, Ash," James replied.

"Oh, look, our host Jason Spark is about to make an appearance," Quentin said while pointing to the stage in the center of the dining hall and looking intently at the stage. The entire dining hall went silent.

A tall man with acne walked out with a mic in hand and said, "Good evening, ladies and gentlemen. I'm your host for the rest of the cruise, Jason Spark. It is such as delight to have you all here on the maiden voyage of the USS Carr. The next week on our way to Fiji will be such an amazing experience for me and I hope for you all, too. Please note that this ship isn't very large, so if you are prone to motion sickness, please come to the main desk later and we have some amazing motion sickness pills that we can give you so you can fully enjoy your vacation. Now, the captain tells me we have a huge assortment of food, drinks, and entertainment for you to enjoy. So I shouldn't take any more of your time, but just wanted to reiterate how excited I am that you are here to celebrate with me. I hope to get to know each of you personally and I hope some of you will invest in us and some of you might just have fun, but all of you will hopefully have some everlasting experiences from this trip. Without further ado, please enjoy the rest of your evening and if you need anything at all, do not hesitate to ask. Thank you all and have a great time!"

With that said, Jason went and sat back down on the captains table. The food was being delivered and it was exquisite. All sorts of cuisines from Italy to Japan to China to India to Mexico to even South African were being delivered to every table. Quinton got out his fork and knife and carefully began to eat his meal like a proper gentleman. Samantha and James, on the other hand, were so confused because they saw pizza and wanted to eat it like normal human beings, but looked at each other and with a shrug decided to "act proper" and eat with a fork and knife.

Samantha couldn't stop talking. She needed to ask everyone everything. She began by talking to Ash. "So why are you here, what is your story?", Samantha asked.

Ash replied, "I honestly just got here because my friend had an extra cruise ticket and I really need a break. So I'm a psychiatrist and honestly I've been getting a ton of these random patients that I'm really really worried might be serial killers, but got to try helping as much as I can, right? I mean, I got a Ted Bundy type, Hannibal Lector type, like it's bad." Then he looked at Quentin as he just realized something. "Wait, Quentin, you're a detective, you must have seen a ton of serial killers, right?"

"I have, but honestly, serial killers make for a terrible story. Their motivation is just so different and, frankly, boring. Now the killers who become killers for a reason and who wouldn't ever resort to murder in other conditions, those are interesting. What makes them tick? Would they have considered murder ever if that one event just never occurred? Maybe it was a lover's quarrel, maybe a robbery gone wrong, maybe it was a cold-blooded vengeance murder, but what if the quarrel never happened, the robbery or the reason for the robbery never happened, the original event never happened so no need for vengeance? Could all those murders have been prevented if we were all normal good human beings? Or would those murders still occur, regardless? Who knows? I've been trying to figure it out my entire life.

"Serial killers, they will continue to kill no matter what. They do have various types of inciting events that start them on their spree, but then you get into a psychological trigger that then profiles and defines the person. There's no way of preventing a serial murder other than catching the killer and improving access to mental health care. Meanwhile, non-serial murders are well-defined, able to be analyzed in and of itself. The perpetrator typically had a connection with the victim of some kind; it isn't a killing spree, generally. It is able to be analyzed from a more analytical lens unlike serial murders that one can get lucky if they find an eyewitness or some forensic evidence, but otherwise have to rely on profiles to eventually catch them since the connection between the victim and perpetrator can be something as simple as appearance, something they said, and sometimes not even anything. Hence, serial killers are boring and vague, but other 'normal' killers, quite interesting," Quentin explained.

Samantha was intrigued and asked, "So can you tell us a story of one of your cases?"

"I definitely can. Actually, I'm going to tell you about a case I never solved," Quentin said ominously and then began.

"So this was back in quarantine, a few years ago. Do you remember the pandemic? Well, I was stuck in a hotel for a few days. And the hotel was a relatively large, upscale hotel so we had a lot of high-profile guests with their own problems, especially this one 70-year-old billionaire who just seem to attract every single bit of wrong attention. On the first night, we all have dinner together somewhat like now actually, and, just like in every detective story, the next day, the housekeeping staff found a man dead. So of course, since I had some experience in this, I immediately went and shut down the whole crime scene and since it was a pandemic, no one could come in or out for the time we were there. We were all stuck with a cold blooded murderer among us for the next few days."

Everyone was hooked, no one could move from their seats, all semblance of dinner forgotten. Quentin continued.

"So the crime scene was immaculate. There was not a single hair out of place. All there was was a dead body on the bed who had been strangled. No murder weapon, no one was immediately a suspect, and literally zero clues to follow. I was at my wit's end. I had no idea how I was going to solve this. So I started where every detective starts, at the crime scene. I inspected every single inch of the crime scene and it was thrilling. There was zero evidence anywhere, which suggested that this was the work of a very very intelligent killer. I then sat down and start interrogating every single resident of that hotel. And they all remembered one thing that night: there was one very skinny man with a very obvious pimple on his left cheek. Now given his description, it should be easy. I mean, how many people out there were skinny and have such a large pimple? And so I started looking everywhere for this guy, and he couldn't be found. It was almost as if he never existed."

"—Is this story time?" A voice came from behind Samantha.

Samantha screamed, "It's him. It's the murderer." Everyone turned and looked and a man walked up.

"Hi everyone, I'm Danny," he said.

Everyone breathed a sigh of relief and then started yelling at Danny.

"Dude, you scared us. Haven't you heard of not interrupting a murder mystery story? You could have given us a heart attack!" Ash exclaimed.

"I'm sorry. I didn't know. What story?" Danny enquired.

"I can't tell it like Quentin, but basically pandemic, guy died, suspect not found, investigation in process," Samantha summarized.

"Please continue, Quentin. Hopefully, no more interruptions," Ash said with a glare at Danny.

Quentin's eyes narrowed and then he continued with his audience holding onto every one of his words. "This person was nowhere to be found. I started wondering if we were led on a wild goose chase. After all, no one can be that memorable; it had to be a disguise. I then interrogated every single person again and of course, every single person had motive to want the rich guy dead and none of them had alibis. You see, he was a tech mogul, and he was ruthless. He had millions of disgruntled employees, some of which were family members of some of the residents. His competition suffered and so most of the other high profile guests wanted him dead because he ruined their business. Finally, the last few guests had their business ventures expanded now that he was out of the way. You had revenge and money working side-by-side as motive for everybody. So great, everybody had motive and opportunity. They were all also stronger than a 70-year-old so they all had means, too. And no physical evidence to go on. Not even the murder weapon. It was the perfect crime, or so the murderer thought."

Quentin took a breath and everyone held their breath in, too, waiting, waiting, waiting. James thought, *he was always a showman, just couldn't resist*. And then he continued.

"So what do I do, you ask? I revisit the crime scene. There must be something there, anything. And then it struck me. It was too perfect. No one can be that perfect. In fact, the room was so clean, it was as if no one had ever lived there. Not even the dead man. Then I realized I had been searching in the wrong place, the crime had never happened there. Have you ever heard of the curious incident of the dog in the nighttime?" Quentin asked.

Everyone stared back blankly, not having a clue. Samantha said, "I haven't heard anything, but I love dogs, so any incident with a dog must be cool."

James and Ash looked at each other, nodding, agreeing with Samantha's statement. *Dogs are cool, but I have no idea the importance of this*, James thought.

Quentin sighed and explained, "so it is a Sherlock Holmes quote from one of his stories. Basically, the story's premise for those who don't know is that there was a home intrusion, but the main clue that cracked the case open was the curious incident of the dog in the nighttime. The dog didn't bark and remained quiet. Now, if it was a true home intrusion, the dog would bark, but since it didn't, it knew the perpetrator. It was the *lack of* evidence that completely opened the case. It was the same thing here.

"My crime scene became the whole hotel. It could have happened anywhere at any time. But then, there were two main questions. Obviously, who did it? But also, when and how did they bring the body back into the room without leaving a single shred of evidence? I started getting into the mind of the killer, feeling what they would have felt, thinking how they would have thought. This can't have been a crime of passion, it was too clean. So how did someone premeditate this? None of us knew the other guests here. And it happened the first day. So someone knew he was going to be here and followed him here. And so then, my search began for this person. Who could have known where he was going to be, who could have followed him, and most importantly, why go to such lengths? So I —"

"Hey guys, just wondering, did you see Jason, yet?" Danny interrupted again.

Ash looked like he was about to become a murderer himself. "Dude, what are you? First you come late, now you're distracting from the story by asking useless questions like have we seen Jason? What's more important, seeing a random guy or finding out who the murderer was?"

"Hey, the story was getting kind of slow, no offense Quentin. I mean come on, we get the general process. We've all watched CSI and Sherlock. We know how mysteries go. You investigate, you find nothing, then something hits you, and then you get in the mind of the killer. Then, you find a final clue, and boom there's the killer. We get it," Danny said.

"Well, go ahead and leave if you don't want to hear it because the rest of us do," Ash replied caustically.

"No, that's not what I meant—"

"No no, go on, there's many tables for dinner. We'll stay with CSI and Sherlock, you can go on with Silicon Valley over there," Ash continued while pointing at the head table where Jason was.

"No, really, it's okay. I would rather get to know you guys. I just really wanted to see Jason, again. " Danny said.

"Wait, what do you mean, again?" Quentin asked.

"Oh, umm, did I say again?" Danny said, looking flustered.

"Uh yeah, you did," Ash responded.

Danny looked like he was going to strangle himself. "Well, I used to work with Jason back in the day. So, again."

"Quentin, if you want me to move the interloper interruptor from our table without leaving any evidence, just say the word," Ash said.

Quentin looked deep in thought.

Is he actually considering it? Or is he thinking about something else? James wondered.

"Hey, uhh, Quentin, sorry to rush you here, but we're all dying to know what happened next" Samantha said. James looked around, everyone had stopped eating and were just looking at the Quentin, Ash, and Danny triangle.

"Yes, sorry. I was just thinking something," Quentin answered.

Quentin took a second, ate another bite of pizza, drank some water, cleared his throat, and soaked in all the attention. After an eternity, he continued.

"So I started interviewing his staff to find anybody who knew his schedule. And they told me one person had asked for a potential meeting with him in order to discuss some business opportunity on that day and they had told that person that he was going to be in this town. I immediately knew this had to be our guy. So now, you see, this hotel had a very exclusive clientele, generally. Most bookings have to happen weeks in advance as the hotel is consistently sold out. That is, unless you are a 70-year old tech billionaire with a trillion connections. It was a long shot, but I went to the hotel manager and asked for details of anybody who had booked just two days before and only one name came up: Jonathan Ember. Obviously a pseudonym, but who knows these days? Who am I to assume? So I went to the room and it was deserted. All that was there was a card saying *Catch me later*."

After saying this, Quentin took out the card from his pocket. "I've been carrying this with me ever since. It is a reminder of the one who got away. The case still remains unsolved to this day."

And with that ominous ending, everyone began eating in silence.

***

After dinner, James decided to take a stroll around the ship. As he turned the corner from the dining room, he bumped into a girl. "I'm so sorry," James said. "No,

I'm sorry, I should have paid attention to where I walking," the girl replied. James got a better look at her, she was considerably tall and carried herself with an air of confidence in herself.

"Hi, I'm Rita. I couldn't believe when I got the invitation for this cruise. I remember it as if it was yesterday. Oh wait, it was yesterday. I was just sitting around, listening to music. By the way, have you heard this new song, I don't know if you listen to Indian songs, but it's so hype. Wait, I'll tell my story first, but then I'll show you my Indian playlist. I think you'll like it. So, yeah, I was just chilling and listening to music when I got an email saying I was invited on this cruise. I was like nahhh, that's a scam, there's no way. Who would invite me to a cruise, right? But then, I checked the authenticity of the email, and it was legit. I was like huh, why? I'm just a regular economist who runs a part time feminist blog on the side. After all, I have to help wherever I can. And then, I got an email from Jason Spark himself explaining the invitation, saying he was really impressed with my work as an economist, and wanted to sit down and meet me to discuss economics. I've only ever read of him, so I was super intrigued, and decided to come. I'm so happy I came though, it is so much fun, I absolutely love this ship. What about you? I hope I didn't just bother you with all these details. I'm sorry if I did. You know what, I'm just going to stop talking now," she said in about ten seconds.

James was stunned. He began to wonder where the mute or pause button was on her. After thirty seconds of awkward silence where James was trying to gather his thoughts, James replied, "Hi, I'm James. I actually just came here with my friend Quentin, he got the invitation cause he's a renowned detective."

Out of nowhere, another girl ran into both of them. "Ahhh, I'm so sorry. I really should watch where I'm going, I'm terribly sorry," she said anxiously.

"No worries, it's completely okay. Hi, I'm James and this is Rita," James replied.

"Hi, I'm Sarah. I'm sorry I'm so flustered, I barely made it on the ship today. You must all think I'm such a nervous wreck" she said while laughing nervously.

Nervous is an understatement to describe her. What a weird cast of characters on this ship, James thought.

"No of course not, you're perfectly fine. I know exactly what you mean. James was just talking about his detective friend, someone named Quentin?" Rita said.

"Yeah, you can't miss him. Electric blue hair, monocle, British, thinks he's god's gift to humanity. What more do you need?" James replied.

"Oh you mean that guy who's walking behind you?" Sarah asked.

James turned around to see Quentin walking up to them, interest sparking in his eyes.

"Oh I see you've met more people, James. Care to introduce me?" Quentin asked.

"Sure, this is Rita and this is Sarah. I just ran into them, literally," James replied.

"Rita, how's the blog going? And congratulations on your cousin's wedding last week! Sarah, I'm really sorry that you had to work so close to your vacation and I really hope Stanford is paying you well for all your work in drug discovery," Quentin commented.

Both Rita and Sarah's mouths dropped open. For once, Rita couldn't come up with words and Sarah stopped shaking nervously because of the shock. *Quentin just loves to do this, show off,* James thought grumpily.

Eventually, Rita got her voice back. "How…how did you know that about me? I just met you!"

Sarah followed, asking "even me? Have we met before?"

"Oh no, of course not. I'm really pleased to meet you both. I'm a detective, observing is what I do," Quentin said proudly.

"Did you stalk me? There's no way you could just observe that," Rita asked. Her eyes showed pure curiosity with no hint of anger.

"Alright, I can explain it to both of you. So I'll start with Rita. You were a bit easier. I actually know your blog; I like to keep up with as many sources of information as I can and I find your blog really well-written and informative. It possesses some new insights I never would have thought of on my own. Of course, I didn't know it was your blog until now. You see, you're wearing a shirt with the logo of the blog. So obviously, you're connected to the blog somehow. Since it's pretty small, there's only a few authors I've noticed. Your name doesn't match any of them and the blog itself doesn't have any merchandise. So that leaves only one possibility, you're the owner and manager of the blog. On top of that, your water bottle has a sticker of an organization of entrepreneurs, specifically in the blog realm. This just confirmed my previous guess. Of course, it could be unrelated, but chances are that it connects with you being the owner and manager of the blog, making it your blog.

"The wedding was a little more lucky. I noticed the henna patterns on your hands. Now, I know that one of the most common occasions that warrants henna are Indian weddings. It could be other festivals too, but your watch has been set to the wrong date, almost as if you set it forward, but when you got back, you didn't move the time back, you continued to set it forward because you forgot about the date. Only way that would happen is if you traveled recently to the other side of the world, around a twelve hour time difference, which would put you in India. That sequence of events felt too unlikely to be a coincidence, hence wedding in India," he said.

"Well, I could have just set the date wrong initially and not gone anywhere," Rita mentioned.

"That's true. Chances are you didn't though. When you set the time on a watch, how would you get the date wrong? Especially because the watch looks decently old, say around a few years, which would mean you would have the wrong date for a few years? And you still wouldn't have fixed it? It seems unlikely," Quentin answered.

"Well you're right about all of that. How? This is insane. How did you figure out that it was a week ago? And how did you know it was my cousin's?" Rita asked.

"The henna pattern has begun to fade significantly, which would put it at around 8-10 days old, hence the last week. The cousin was a lucky guess. I guessed it wasn't yours because I would have imagined you would be on your honeymoon right now or if this is your honeymoon, you would have brought your husband and not been walking around at night alone. Sure, you could have been walking out at night for fresh air or he's asleep or some other unforeseen reason I haven't thought of yet, but the chances are far less likely. Now, I doubt you would travel all the way to India for a friend, so it is likely to be a family member. Given my general estimate of your age around the mid 20s, it's unlikely that the wedding was that of an uncle or aunt. Of course, it could definitely happen, but again, generally unlikely. You probably have dozens of cousins, but only a few siblings, so more likely to be a cousin than a sibling. That leaves the most likely possibility as a cousin, so I just guessed. A huge part of deducing from observations is guessing and using probability to your advantage. You would be wrong many times, but you'll be right more often than not, which is the key," Quentin explained.

"That is amazing. I cannot believe you got that just from

looking at me for a few seconds," Rita said still completely shocked.

"What about me? How did you figure out all the things about me?" Sarah asked bewildered.

"Well to begin with, I noticed those marks around your eyes. Those are lab safety goggle marks. On top of that, your hands have mild burns that look consistent with boiling water and marks of acid that has irritated your skin. Each of these marks are very recent, probably between four hours and two hours ago. Now, I know the ship has left dock two and a half hours ago, which would mean you were working at max 90 minutes before the ship left. I knew you were thus likely a chemist from those marks. Recently ever since the pandemic, there's been a huge increase in drug discovery jobs compared to other jobs in chemistry, so I took a chance that you work in drug discovery. Finally, given you were working 90 minutes before the ship left, you must be very close by, probably within a 20-30 minute drive to be able to get from your lab to your car and drive here to make it in time to get through security to get onto the ship. The only large institute within a 20-30 minute drive is Stanford, so thus, you likely work at Stanford in drug discovery," Quentin answered.

"That's exactly right. Wow, I still cannot believe it. James, your friend here is not just a detective, he's a magician," Sarah said.

Yeah, he shows off more than a magician, too. He had no actual need to get into this; he just likes to to prove he's a detective on par with Sherlock Holmes, James thought.

"Anyway, it was great meeting you both. I hope to see you around the ship over the next week," Quentin said and began to walk to his room.

James then looked at his watch and noticed the time, it was way past his bedtime. "Sorry guys, I would love to talk more, but I just saw the time and I think I will need to retire early.

But like Quentin, I'll see both of you around over the next seven days, for sure," James stated.

He then made his way back to his room, thinking to himself, *Wow, what a bunch of strange people on this cruise. I wonder what the next seven days have in store for us. Something feels weird about this whole cruise. I mean, this isn't your general audience of high class people, is it? Ash is a psychiatrist, Danny feels like someone random who worked with Jason in the past. Samantha is a photographer, Sarah a chemist, Rita an economist. There's almost zero connection between any of them, except that they all don't scream rich. And then there is Quentin and me, we're on a whole other level of weird. After all, why would Quentin be invited? Who even invited him and by proxy me? The only rich person I've seen so far is Jason himself and he disappeared so quickly too. Some host he is. I don't know. I guess we'll figure out what's going on sooner or later.*

***

The next day, James and Quentin made their way to breakfast where they saw a pompous young man eating bread with a fork and knife. Quentin whispered to James, "this has to lead to an exciting conversation. What a weird fellow."

Quentin's calling someone weird? James wondered.

Quentin came up to him and asked, "Can my associate and I have the pleasure of sitting here and having breakfast with you?"

The man replied, "Of course you can have the pleasure of sitting with *moi*."

James never saw Quentin so excited about the prospect of having a conversation. *I wonder why he's so excited about this guy. I've only seen that look before when he wants to set someone up or to mess with them. If that's true, at least this will be an eventful conversation,* James thought.

"Hi, I'm Quentin Vance. I'm the world's greatest detective. This is James," Quentin introduced.

"Hello, I am Aldrich Appleton, the world's premier businessman and one of the wealthiest residents of the greatest country in the world, the United Kingdom of Great Britain and Northern Ireland," Aldrich replied.

"Do you ever use any contractions, by chance, or maybe slang, or just something other than proper English?" Quentin queried.

"Of course not, I will only use the Queen's English, and no other form of improper English. It is an insult to such a beautiful and pristine language to speak in anything else," Aldrich replied while dabbing at his mouth with his napkin. *What is this guy? Which planet did he come from? Well obviously, he says he came from England, but he's got to be an alien? There's no way people like this are real, right?* James thought.

"My, aren't you pretentious?" Quentin said rhetorically.

"Of course I am, I am the most pretentious man you will ever meet," Aldrich said with pride. James was surprised. *Does he even know what pretentious means, or is he truly proud of being pretentious? I cannot understand this guy*, he thought.

"I bet you are iniquitous and are Hippopotomonstrosesquipedaliophobic, too," Quentin said, laughing to himself. "Yes, I am, how did you know?" Aldrich replied. Quentin couldn't contain his laughter anymore and excused himself and left the room. "What an interesting character," Aldrich said to James.

James was so lost in this conversation. *Quentin is an interesting character, yes, but this specimen has to have him beat*, he thought. He then shook his head as if to clear his thoughts and then said, "yes, that he is. Please excuse me, I'll go check on him."

James then got up and left the room to follow Quentin. He found Quentin in the hallway right next to the dining room, doubled over in laughter. "I don't get it, what's funny?" James asked.

"That person just cracks me up. I mean, he's obviously rich, I don't doubt it. But, did you see the way he was acting? He was 100% raised into wealth. He truly doesn't know what not having money is like. On top of that, I don't think he's all that bright, but he loves acting like he is. Probably stems from some insecurity about him and his company, which I wonder about. The name sounds familiar, too. Anyway, did you get what I was saying?" Quentin replied.

"No, I'm actually lost. I mean I know what pretentious means and I gather he didn't know, but thought it was a compliment when it clearly wasn't. But I don't know what you said afterwards," James answered.

"Well, so iniquitous means evil. It's supposed to represent like morally wrong, so obviously he didn't know that or he wouldn't have agreed to it. Hippopotomonstrosesquipedaliophobic means having a fear of big words. I think you can appreciate the irony there," Quentin responded.

James thought to himself, *well, I do appreciate the irony. But also I don't think that this is really all that funny. Quentin sure has a weird sense of humor. But at the end, I was right. It was an eventful conversation. I wonder what will happen in the future with him, something about him just screams different and unusual, and it's not just his pompous pretentious attitude.*

***

Later that day, James was walking to dinner when he passed Rita, who was muttering to herself. "Can't believe it... ignorant pig...all men are dogs...Jason Spark is the most sexist man I've ever met," she was mumbling angrily. *I wonder what happened to her, she was so cheery yesterday,* James thought.

"Hey Rita, how is everything going? I'm headed to dinner, want to join me?" James asked.

Rita brightened up and said, "Hi James, I'm fine,

everything's fine, all's good. I would, but actually, I have some work to do first, I might join you later?"

"Alright, I'll see you around then," said James and headed to dinner.

At dinner, James saw Quentin sitting next to Danny and two other men who he had never seen before and joined them.

"Hey James, you already know Danny. This is Ron and Aron," Quentin introduced.

"Hi everyone, I'm James, in case you didn't catch Quentin just introducing me," James replied.

"Come, let's eat, I'm famished," Quentin said.

The food began being served all around the table. Quentin sat with his usual fork and knife, methodically cutting into his lasagna. Danny and Ron looked at each other and began tearing into their steak. Aron was taking pictures of the dining room while his pizza began to get cold. James was marveling at the sight of such a busy dining room. On the table next to them, Ash, Samantha, and Sarah were talking fervently, their food almost untouched.

"Hey guys," James called out to them. They stopped mid conversation to see who was calling from a different table and saw James and waved.

Then, Ash picked up his food and came over to their table. "Hey James and Quentin, can we join you guys?"

"Of course, there's more than enough room, and the more, the merrier. Please have a seat," Quentin replied. The three of them brought their food over and sat down excitedly. *The table looks so busy and diverse all of a sudden. Over on one end, Danny and Ron were in an engaged conversation about computer science. On this end, Samantha, Sarah, Ash, and Aron were engaged in gossip. Quentin is just sitting there, observing everything like a hawk,* James noticed.

"So guys, you want to hear a story about Aron and I back

in college?" Samantha asked.

"Wait, you knew each other back in college?" James replied.

"Yeah, we were in all the same classes and clubs. Especially in regards to photography, we constantly were competing against each other," Aron answered.

"I was definitely the better photographer," Samantha declared.

"As if, I had you beat on so many of those aesthetic photos," Aron shot back.

"Anyway, you were saying, some story?" Ash interrupted.

"Oh yeah, so this was freshman year. We had joined this photo competition. The grand prize was a thousand dollars. It was a treasure hunt where we had to take pictures of every location, which led to a new clue. Finally, after the final picture was taken of the final location, you would submit the portfolio and get points for each picture. You would get points for it being the correct location and the aesthetic quality of the picture. The final picture was worth twice the points. Finally, the faster you submit the portfolio, the greater the time bonus you got," Samantha explained.

"We get the rulebook Samantha. What actually happened?" Sarah interrupted.

"Well, Aron and I both got to the final location really quickly and took the picture at around the same time. Then, exactly as we were going to upload the portfolio, Aron's phone died and he didn't have a portable charger around him. By the time he managed to charge his phone and upload the portfolio, I had already submitted it. When the final scores came out, we tied even after the time bonus I received. I don't even know what they saw in his pictures," Samantha continued.

"Hey, my pictures were golden. If my phone didn't die, I would be the one telling the story," Aron declared.

"Well, it did die right? And the tiebreaker, wait for it, was the time bonus, so I won the prize, all one thousand dollars," Samantha finished.

"What I wouldn't give for a thousand dollars, right now," Aron muttered under his breath. James looked around at everyone else and saw blank faces. He made eye contact with Quentin and Quentin slightly nodded, indicating he had heard Aron as well.

"Sorry what was that Aron?" Sarah asked.

"Oh nothing, not important," replied Aron, his face turning red.

"No offense, Samantha. That wasn't a very interesting story," Danny commented.

"Dude, you say that about everything. You said that about Quentin's hotel killer and this. If you find them so boring, why don't you just leave and find another table then? Why are you even here?" Ash replied angrily.

"That's not what I meant, I don't want to leave you guys," replied Danny hastily.

"I don't see you having any stories. If you have any interesting stories, we're all ears. Do you?" Ash challenged.

Danny fell silent and slumped back in his chair. *Wow, this is the second time Ash shot Danny down. He's really not afraid to speak his mind and defend people, is he?* James thought. *But he did bring up a valid point, why is Danny even here? He's never contributing to a conversation, he's just content to be an observer.*

"So anyway, Aron, are you here to get a picture with Jason Spark as well?" Samantha asked.

"Yeah, of course. And I will win this time, I have to," Aron answered defiantly.

"We'll see, you already lost once. Just give up, already," Samantha replied confidently.

James watched the two of them bicker back and forth and then began to observe the rest of the table. Danny and Ron began talking again with each other. Quentin was eating slowly, carefully looking at the rest of the table as well. Sarah started shaking from the cold in the room and was looking disinterested in the Aron-Samantha Photography Cup, constantly looking at her watch. Ash was watching the contest unfold, but was particularly looking at Samantha. Time began to dilate slowly while this all continued. James began to be lulled into a lethargic rhythm with the constant noise around him fading away until it was just a light buzzing, as if it was a white noise machine.James could hear the ticking of his watch, slowly counting out every second of every minute that was passing. He heard it hit 7 o'clock just as slowly and peacefully as everything around him was unfolding.

—BANG! There was a loud noise that startled everyone, even Quentin. A body came flying down into the dining hall. Quentin immediately looked up to see the origin of the body and saw a balcony that opened into the dining hall with a curtain fluttering and a shadow moving behind it. "Oh come on, I was eating," Quentin complained as he ran towards the balcony climbing up the stairs to that floor, five at a time. He was followed by Aron and Ron. When he reached the room, he broke down the door to find that there was nobody there. Whatever the shadow was, it was gone.

He then went back to the dining hall to assess the scene. Sarah was screaming, Samantha was stunned, Ash was scrambling to see who the body was. Danny was quivering. "Everyone, aside, now. I'm Quentin Vance, a detective. I will figure out everything that is going on. Move aside," Quentin yelled. He walked to the body, a skinny man, who had a fair complexion, some acne, and was 6'6". He fell on his front with a gunshot wound to his back and some bruising around his arm. Quentin called Aron over and took his camera to take pictures of the crime scene. Then, he turned the body on its back so he could see his face. Sarah screamed, "It's Jason Spark!"

3

Chaos ensued. Everyone started running and screaming. Quentin immediately jumped on a table. "Everyone, stop where you are, please, and move away from the body," he ordered in a commanding tone that got everyone's attention. Everyone froze. Sarah was looking at Ash who was looking at Samantha who was looking at the body. After a few seconds of it sinking in, Samantha and Aron threw up simultaneously. Danny looked stricken. *Oh right, Danny knew Jason from before. No wonder he looks so shocked*, James realized.

"I can't believe Jason died. Is this some sick prank?" Ron asked.

"He definitely died, I can't imagine this convoluted of a prank. Plus I thought this cruise would be too fancy for such a cheap prank," Aron replied.

"Did he just fall out of the window or was he pushed?" Danny asked.

"He definitely got this gigantic hole in his chest and back from falling down the stairs. How about I put you in the balcony and push you over the railing and we'll see the hole in your chest. We can even see who has the bigger wound and give out a prize," Ash replied sarcastically. Danny gulped and stopped talking. *Wow, Ash really has it out for Danny, doesn't he? Even after someone died, he's not going to let him go,* James realized.

"Wait this means someone killed him?" Ron asked.

"Yeah, a gunshot typically implies someone killed him," Samantha replied.

"Do you guys know what this means? One of us on the ship is a cold-blooded murderer," Sarah proclaimed ominously, still shaking. Everyone immediately stopped talking and became dead silent.

Quentin took this opportunity to call the captain of the ship. "Hey, could you lock down the dining room and ensure that nobody can leave the ship until we get to the bottom of this. When we get back to port, I want to have the murderer in custody. Also, make sure no one other than James and I go into Jason's room. Not even housekeeping." The captain proceeded to lock down the dining room and move everyone out of the room back to their rooms.

He then decided to go upstairs to Jason's room. James followed in tow along with Ash, Samantha, and Sarah.

Quentin observed the room. The door was busted from when Quentin broke it down. The bolt on the door was broken as well. The room itself was trashed. The king size bed was ruffled in one corner of the room. The sofa was pushed to the middle of the room. There was fishing line in another corner of the room near an old-fashioned clock with some of the line going all over the room to the door and the chair. The TV was moved to be near the bed. In another corner, there was a slightly opened case of fireworks. Near the balcony, there was an overturned chair next to a lone firework. There was a huge spatter of blood in the middle of the room, in which there were no footprints despite the spatter spilling all over the room and over the furniture. Jason's computers were all turned off and all over the desk.

When Quentin went to turn the computers on, he found that they were all wiped. "Hmm, interesting," Quentin said to himself. He then noticed something out of the corner of his eye: Ash had bent down and picked up something and put it in his pocket and then left the room. *My, my, this has now become even more interesting*, Quentin thought.

"Hey guys, can you go back to your rooms? I need to make sure the crime scene isn't compromised," Quentin stated. Sarah and Samantha looked ashamed and then proceeded to follow Ash out.

"James, did you just see what I saw?" Quentin asked.

"Nope, you know I never see what you see, what did you see on this day out at sea?" James replied, laughing to himself at his pun. He thought it was genius.

Quentin groaned inwardly. "Ash picked up something from the crime scene and left. He's definitely hiding something, we'll find out what when we interrogate them," Quentin said.

Quentin then turned his attention back to the state of the room and started walking around and started knocking on the wall, listening intently.

"I'm so confused, Quentin. How did the killer even enter this room, you said it was locked and bolted. I mean, look at the door, it's completely destroyed, including the bolt. Even if, let's say Jason let the killer in, maybe it was someone he knew, how did the killer escape? There's only two ways out of this room, the door that you destroyed and the balcony that Jason destroyed. He obviously couldn't leave out the door you destroyed, or it wouldn't have been bolted, and he obviously didn't leave out the balcony, or we would have seen him while eating dinner. I'm so lost. Please tell me you got something I didn't," James said.

Quentin was deep in thought and barely listening. *Oh, great, he's now thinking and when he thinks, he doesn't talk,* James thought. Quentin finished walking around the room and then snapped back to attention and looked at James and replied, "Hmm, you are correct. How could the killer leave or enter? I wonder…" *Wonderful, he is now wondering,* James thought irritably.

Quentin then decided to go on one of his observation rants. James could see Quentin's blue hair standing up and his monocle quivering with Quentin's excitement, *Here we go, he's gearing up in 3, 2, 1.*

Quentin began, "Alright so what we have here is an unusual crime scene. As you so astutely pointed out, there is no way for the killer to leave. So there are two major possibilities in front of us, either the killer is still here or there is a secret passage. However, I'm loathe to believe either of them because of the scene we have in front of us. There is no evidence that the killer has hidden, and I don't think he would have, simply because it is too risky. He would know that we would come up here and probably lock the room from the outside and he would be stuck. He can't be that stupid. That leaves the secret passage. While the secret passage is technically possible, the likelihood that it exists is tiny because this is a brand new ship, where a secret passage is not required. There is absolutely no reason to have one. Why would Jason Spark need to run when in theory, the ship's security is top notch. At the same time, all the walls of this room are completely solid, I have already checked. There is no place where a secret passage could exist. So that leaves a third possibility, which I have no idea, yet, but that's the fun, isn't it?

"Now, on to the rest of the scene. First, you'll notice the place is trashed. That's obvious. What you will notice if you look closer is that the place is *systematically* trashed. When was the last time you moved a sofa to search for something? And if you were to move a sofa to maybe look for something underneath it, you wouldn't expend extra energy to move it almost 15 feet into the middle of the room. Doesn't make sense, does it? Of course not. This leads me to believe that the place was trashed to give the appearance that the killer was looking for something to make us believe either this was a simple robbery or that the motive was to find something. Maybe the killer wanted us to believe that Jason Spark walked in on the killer searching for something and then they struggled, which led to the gun firing. So obviously that did not occur, which means the motive was something else, something more personal. This wasn't just an accident. This also shows the killer having a strange sense of bravery. An afraid person won't hang around after brutally murdering someone to move everything around. It's not easy to create this level of mess in short time.

"Next, let's look at the computers. The computers are completely wiped. There's only two reasons why the computers would be wiped: one, the computers contained some evidence of motive or something that could incriminate the killer, or two, this was a case of corporate espionage. Of course, the killer could be bluffing, but that would mean he wasted valuable time to wipe computers that he didn't need, which seems implausible to me. Therefore, we should consider the first two possibilities especially when we look at motives later.

"Finally, let's look at the elephant in the room, the elephant-sized blood spatter in the middle of the room. There's no footprints. This means we are looking for a very careful and methodical killer, someone who has the presence of mind after shooting a man in cold blood to walk carefully around the gigantic blood spatter to avoid leaving prints. Moreover, where's the murder weapon? We don't have a gun or even a shell casing. The killer must have taken both with him when he left, that is another thing we must find out. So much to do, come, let us go into my room to write out a timeline of what we know happened and then we can bring in everybody and interrogate them," Quentin said and without waiting for a second, spun around and left the room.

***

"Alright, let's begin the timeline, shall we," Quentin said. They had gone back to Quentin's room and were sitting in the living room section of his room.

"So first, the killer enters the room, presumably by somehow breaking in or Jason let him in. If we assume the former, we have to think that the killer began wiping the computer before Jason came in. In that case, Jason could have surprised the killer, which cause a struggle in which Jason got shot. That struggle caused the whole state of the room. He gets shot, his body falls through the balcony by the force of impact into the dining hall. Then, in those 10-15 seconds, the killer carefully escapes the room, the method TBD, with the door bolted, before we came and broke down the door," James said.

Quentin looked disappointed. "Did you not pay attention during my whole monologue five minutes ago? We had determined that the struggle did not trash the room, the room was made to look trashed, in which case, it was trashed before Jason got shot, which means that Jason was the intended target. The killer wanted to kill Jason beforehand. It was premeditated!!!" Quentin said exasperatedly.

"Ok, ok, don't get your blue hair into a curl, let's assume the latter then. Jason let the killer in. The killer then began to trash the room and wipe the computers and then shot Jason and escaped," James offered.

"And what, Jason just watches and is like go on, I love the way you're destroying my room and taking all my work. You missed a spot over there, don't forget to move the sofa," Quentin commented sarcastically.

"Ok, what about if, ummm, Jason is tied up?" James wondered.

"Maybe, that might just be the closest thing to the truth yet. So Jason was tied up... Except Jason was a pretty big guy so how did the killer get Jason tied up in the first place? Do you think they asked Jason to pretty please sit still while they tie a rope around him?" Quentin asked rhetorically.

Quentin is insufferable when he's in one of these moods. I should just stop talking so I don't somehow further his sarcasm. I'm sorry we're not all supposed to be this great detective used to this. I came to go on a cruise and that's it. It's supposed to be a vacation and instead I'm stuck with Mr. Sarcastic Know-it-all, thought James.

"Well I guess we don't have another theory. So let's say the killer somehow ties up Jason in the chair, then shoots him - bang! Now the body drops, which explains the overturned chair. One observation here. Jason fell on his front and was shot in the back. What killer shoots someone who's tied up facing away from them? Anyway, let's keep going. There's obviously a large noise and everyone runs up. The killer has to leave the room or they'll get caught, and then somehow lock the room. Let's say they do that, somehow. We made it up the stairs rather quickly and because of Jason owning the ship, his hallway is pretty long with no other room in sight. Where could the killer have gone where we didn't see them? It would take a few seconds to run down the hallway, which was the same time it took us to reach the hallway. So physically, the only way the killer could have escaped was if they somehow locked the door and managed to teleport away. Also this is a movie myth, shooting someone does not force them backwards like what Hollywood suggests. It's basic physics. Action = reaction," Quentin said while pacing around the room.

Oh wonderful, now I get to revisit physics. What a delight, James thought.

"The bullet has very little actual momentum because it's so small. When it hits a human being, which is considerably more massive than it, the momentum is transferred, but due to the large mass, there's very little velocity so the person doesn't just get thrown backwards. Plus according to this theory, Jason was restrained. Where's the rope? And if he was restrained, how was he thrown backwards? Kinda defeats the point of restraining, doesn't it?" Quentin stated without slowing his pacing one bit.

"So the only option is the killer shoots him, somehow gets the ropes off him and throws him down where we can all see the murder, basically putting all the focus on him. What murderer does that? How does he do that? There was very little time between the gunshot and the body dropping. Now the killer has to remember to get the rope, the gun, and the shell casing, along with whatever work he stole and escape in less than fifteen seconds. Not to mention lock the door. That's an impressive killer. Either they are very stupid and got lucky or they are purposely taunting me. I really hope it's the latter," Quentin said and stopped pacing and turned to James.

"I'm going to have so much fun catching this one! Let the interrogations begin!" Quentin crowed.

He always had a flair for the dramatic, didn't he?

4

Sarah was the first to enter the room. "Welcome Sarah, please sit down." Quentin said with a grim look on his face.

"I want to confess something," Sarah said. James and Quentin exchanged looks.

"You're the murderer, you killed Jason?" asked James. Sarah nodded her head.

"Are you joking?" Quentin asked.

"No I'm not, I'm serious," Sarah replied as she looked down at her feet. James and Quentin looked at each other again before Quentin spoke again, "Okay well... why don't you tell us what happened?"

Sarah took a deep breath and began, "I did it. I'm the murderer. The guilt is eating me from the inside. I can't hold it in any longer. I hated Jason. He drove me crazy. One day, he had said enough sexist things and so I knocked on his door, entered his room, and then shot him, and ran out."

Quentin was skeptical. "What did you do with the murder weapon?"

"I threw it overboard," she replied.

"How did you bolt the door behind you?" Quentin persisted.

"Easy, I used a magnet that I later then also threw

overboard," she replied while looking anxiously around.

"Okay, so tell me all that you did yesterday, spare no detail."

"Can you tell me exactly how you killed him, where you got the gun, and what time was all this?"

"Well, umm…I brought the gun with me, you know for protection. At that point, I knocked on his door, as I said, then ran in, shot him …in the heart? Then I cleaned up the crime scene, ran out, locked the door with the magnet, and then threw the gun and magnets overboard. This was all at 7:00 PM?"

"A few more questions, sorry. What about the knife wound on his leg? And I thought you were with us at dinner at 7? And what did his room look like when you left it"

"Oh, I must have forgotten about the knife wound." After a brief pause, she said, "Right, I remember now. When he saw me coming with a gun, he took out his knife and came at me, but when I shot him, the knife must have cut his leg as he fell. And was I with you at 7? Well, then, umm, this must have been right before that, I must have mixed up the time. His room was normal, I guess? Nothing special"

"Okay, so why are you even on this cruise?"

"Well, I just got this email. You see, I'm a chemist. Do you remember the pandemic a few years ago? I helped discover the cure for it. So Jason emailed me, saying he was impressed with my work with that, as the pandemic had ruined his company, and wanted to invite me here for free to thank me. And then he never did, but instead kept saying how girls couldn't discover the cure to anything, except an empty stomach! Like seriously? I've been constantly fighting criticism my entire life because no one believes girls can be chemists, and the guy whose company I helped supposedly save, who gave me a free ticket to the cruise, is insulting me? I had to snap," she finished heatedly.

"You helped cure the pandemic? I remember that. It was terrible, I couldn't leave my house for months. That's unbelievable, you literally saved the world," James said astonished.

"I agree with James, that's quite the feat. Alright, you may go now. If there is anything else, we will let you know," Quentin dismissed. Sarah spun around and marched out.

After the door closed, James looked at Quentin, stunned. "Why did you let her go, Quentin?"

"Easy, I don't think she did it. Can you guess why?" Quentin asked. James started thinking. "Well, her motive seemed pretty weak. Oh, I got it, is it because she's too obvious? I mean, I've read so many mystery books and it's never the obvious suspect," James said triumphantly.

"Well, you are almost completely wrong, but it's a good try. First, motives aren't weak or strong, everything is dependent on the suspect. Something that might seem weak to us might be very strong to them. For instance, Jason's sexism might not be important enough to us to justify a murder, mainly because we aren't the target of his prejudice. But people who are his target can be affected heavily and you or I would never realize it. Is his murder fair and justified? Maybe, but regardless, our job isn't to analyze if his murder is fair or not, we can leave that to philosophers and the court. So her motive isn't really weak. Never judge someone based on their motive.

"Also, in real life, the most obvious suspect is usually it. We don't get cases like in mystery books where the obvious can be ignored. Normally, the murder isn't very premeditated and the suspect leaves so many clues, it is easy to identify. No, her being obvious isn't why I don't think she did it.

"I think she is lying to protect somebody. I think she saw something, and I'm going to find out. For one, this is a fancy cruise. Have you looked at your door bolt? It is pure silver.

Jason's is pure gold. Gold isn't magnetic at all, she couldn't have used a magnet to lock the door. Second and more importantly, do you remember where she was when we heard the gunshot? She was in the dining hall with us. She has a pretty air-tight alibi. Third, there was no knife wound and I believe she had been lying from the moment she walked through the door. He wasn't shot in the heart, he was shot in the back, there's no way her story holds any water. Her description of the scene was also completely wrong. Finally, remember what we said about the killer? We deduced that the killer is methodical, cold-blooded. This murder was premeditated. Sarah fits none of this. A methodical killer won't confess, and her timeline suggests the murder wasn't premeditated, which we know is false. The one thing I do believe her for is what she said at the end. I truly believe she was angry at Jason, and she had every right to, I just don't believe she's the killer. Let's find out who she's trying to protect," Quentin said and then sat back waiting for the next person.

***

Samantha walked in next. "Let's hope this is a normal interview," muttered James under his breath.

Samantha sat down and said dramatically, "I did it!" James groaned and banged his head against the desk.

Quentin seemed perplexed, which was a first. "What did you do?" He asked.

"Duh, I killed Jason. He was getting on my nerves for the past two days. Like who does he think he is? Yeah, he may be a billionaire, but still, there is something called decency and respect. He kept going around bragging about how he was this awesome guy who was really rich, too. Well, yeah, we know you're rich, you don't need to highlight it. And then the last straw was when I went to ask him for a picture, and he suddenly started acting super scared as if I asked him to donate all his money to charity and become a hermit in the Himalayas. It was just a picture! One picture! He then dismissed me pretty quickly and ran away and that was it, I was angry and went to his room and shot him. It was a pretty good shot too, if I do say so myself, and I don't regret it at all. He got what was coming to him," she replied.

Quentin looked lost in thought. He got up and started pacing, muttering to himself and then shook his head and addressed Samantha, "May I ask around what time this all happened?"

"He ran away maybe an hour or two before dinner and I shot him right before dinner," she replied.

"So that would be around 5:00 PM? Since we had dinner at 7:00 PM," Quentin said.

"Yeah that sounds about right," she responded.

"What about before that, give me a play by play of your entire day."

"Alright so… first, I woke up, got a pretty heavy breakfast. Breakfast is the key to a good day. Then around 10 AM, I saw Hemant walking to the gym. Then I hung around the pool for a bit, I love swimming.

"Okay, now let's go back to Jason. How did you kill him?"

"I shot him? I thought that was pretty obvious considering he died from a gunshot."

"I meant more how you did it, as in the actual mechanics?"

"Well, you put your finger on the trigger and just pull, it's not that hard. Are you sure you're a good detective?"

"Okay just tell me where you got the gun, how you entered his room, killed him, then somehow left the room, locked the door, disposed of the gun, all while you were sitting with us at dinner. Also, how was the state of the room after you left," Quentin said while struggling to remain calm.

"Ohhh, ummm…uhh well I got the gun from him, it was just in the room and I just picked it up then shot him in the chest. Then, I rigged up the chair so it would blast from there out the balcony so it would drop while we are there. And… uhhh…ummm…threw the gun overboard…and just locked the door behind me with a magnet. And then I ran down to join you guys for dinner. That's how I did it! The room was pretty clean overall, well except for the blood where I shot him," Samantha finished triumphantly, looking very pleased with herself.

"Okay…so on another note, why are you here?" Quentin tactfully changed topics.

Stunned, Samantha said, "Why are you asking that? I mean what difference does that make, I just told you I killed a man. You found the person you're looking for."

"Just need to understand some more things."

"Okay… well, let's see here. Umm, so I was sent here, really to get a picture of Jason. It's a running joke among all us photographers that Jason Spark is basically the photography holy grail. That's why Aron's here, too. You know, I've known Aron for a really long time. He's the kind of guy who would do anything for a picture; he's even more competitive than me. It's why we had that running competition for so long now."

"So you didn't know Jason before this trip?"

"Nope, just rumors."

"And because you were *angry*, you shot and killed a man and then tidied up the crime scene?"

"Yep, now I was always very clean so the cleaning was easy."

"Samantha, do you have any experience with computers at all?"

"Like photoshop? Or like computers computers, like Bill Gates computers?"

"Computers computers. I just lost some files and I need to recover them" Quentin said.

47

"Nope, not even a bit. I'm sure there's other people on this ship, after all, Jason was a software mogul."

"Alright, thank you. I'll be on the lookout. That will be all. You may head back to your room, now. We will send for you if needed," Quentin said.

"Huh, you won't hold me in custody or anything?" Samantha seemed confused.

"No, not yet. We need to still talk to everybody on the ship first. Who knows, maybe somebody else confesses?" Quentin laughed inwardly.

Samantha left and James turned to Quentin, confused, "What now? Who actually committed this crime?"

"We will see, this case is shaping up to be really fun. So far, we have two suspects who've confessed, but have concrete alibis as even Samantha was with us during dinner. However, there were two main points from her statement that were interesting, I wonder if you picked up on it," Quentin replied. James was confused, "Her entire statement seemed pointless to me."

"Well, while most of her statement was pointless, you need to learn to listen between the lines. We have now gotten a better idea of a timeline, such as the last time Jason was seen alive for now is 5:00 PM by Samantha. We have also discovered something about our victim, *he hated photos*. That could just be a quirk or something else, I don't know, but it's intriguing for sure."

That's it. Quentin's lost it. How can pictures be interesting? And we already know the timeline, why is he so obsessed? The next person is going to walk in and dramatically say "I did it" just like the rest of the suspects. Maybe everybody did it? Too bad this isn't a train in Europe, but a ship in the Pacific, James thought to himself.

***

Ash walked in, looking somewhat uneasy. *Alright, now, Ash is going to say he did it, too, this is totally a pattern,* James thought. Ash sat down and said, "I did it. I killed Jason Spark."

James groaned and banged his head against the table. "What's his issue?" Ash asked while looking at James. "Ignore him, today's been a pressing day," Quentin replied, "tell me more about what happened."

"So I ran into Samantha and she was complaining about Jason Spark. After hearing about what happened, I decided to go find him and give him a piece of my mind. I went up to his room around 5:15 PM and confronted him. We got into an argument and I found a gun and shot him. I then ran out of there, scared of what I had done. Afterwards, the guilt was just eating me alive. I couldn't handle what I had done so I had to come here to confess," Ash recounted.

"What about the thing you picked up at the edge of the room?" Quentin asked.

"Oh, you saw that, didn't you? Of course you did, you are a detective after all. Yeah, I had just dropped a pin during that whole argument. So I went to go pick it up, that's all."

"How did you find the gun? Where was it?"

"It was just lying around his room. I just got so angry!"

"A few more questions. Where did you shoot him? What did the room look like when you left? And finally, if you shot him at 5:15, why did his body fall during dinner?"

"I shot him in the stomach. His room was pretty trashed up because of the argument. Oh, it must have been after 5:15 then, I'm not entirely sure," he answered.

"Alright, you may go now. If there are any more questions, I will let you know," Quentin dismissed.

After Ash left, James turned to Quentin. "I sincerely hope the next person doesn't try to confess and tries to profess his innocence. Frankly, I'm getting annoyed by this case."

"Quite to the contrary, I feel this case is one of the most interesting yet. You never have a case with a confession, let alone three. The more the merrier, I say, let the next one in," Quentin shouted in glee.

***

Next walked in Rita. "Did you kill him?" asked James, eager to get the confession out of the way this time.

"Huh, what are you talking about? Of course I didn't kill him. Plus, even if I did, am I crazy to tell you that I did?" Rita replied. James laughed inwardly, *if only you knew our day so far, but finally, somebody who didn't do it.*

"Ignore him, James is as forthright as they come. Please, tell me, what's your story?" Quentin interjected.

"So I was born in California. Now, when I was really young, I was very inquisitive. Did you know I ate grass just to see what it tasted like? My parents weren't really happy. And then when I was six months old, I got a dog, and now dogs are amazing, I love dogs. When I turned one year old, I began to walk, slightly late possibly, idk. I started talking at 18 months, and…"

"Ok, stop. Not that story. Why are you on the cruise and what happened the past few days?" Quentin interrupted.

"Ohhhhh, why didn't you say so? I'm so used to giving my whole life story, I was like why do you want to stay here for so long listening to me, but like why not, right? So I started. Either way, I'm an economist. Which you probably already know given our introduction the other day. Apparently, Jason Spark loved my work as an economist and wanted to discuss it with me. I met you guys the other day and that was really it. I did meet this one person, British I think? I'm not sure his name. But he was so rude! So after that, I stayed to myself, wandering the ship. And then, eventually, the incident happened. Honestly, I didn't even know it happened. I just heard a large sound, ran to it, and found everyone in a state of panic," Rita recounted.

"Did you ever interact with Jason Spark?" Quentin asked.

"Nope, actually once, I was supposed to talk with him about economics the day he died. But when I went to his room, it was locked and nobody was answering, so I left. After that, the next time I saw him, he was dead."

James was surprised. He distinctly remembered Rita grumbling the day Jason died and he decided to broach the subject. "Why are you lying? What was the whole deal with Jason Spark being the most sexist man you've ever met?" He asked challengingly.

Rita immediately turned pale and started stumbling. She then took a deep breath and said clearly, "I wasn't being completely honest earlier. I didn't go to his room, but I did interact with him. I knew how it would look, so I lied. I'm sorry."

"Well, okay, so where did you interact with him and what happened?" Quentin asked.

"I was walking around the ship and I ran into Jason in a hallway. I was so excited to see him and began to thank him for the invitation and for appreciating my work and he looked at me with surprise. He said he never invited me and he definitely wouldn't appreciate an economists work. On top of all of it, he said there was no way he would invite a girl, saying he appreciated their work, and that economics is too math-heavy for girls anyway. As you can imagine, I was furious. I yelled at him for a few minutes and ran away. I couldn't imagine that kind of reception ever. I mean now in the 21st century? Aren't we past this whole thing yet? I guess not, especially when someone like Jason Spark still believes that girls can't do math. So yeah, did we fight? Yes. Did I kill him? Definitely not," she answered angrily.

"Alright, final question, where exactly were you when you heard the sound, and why weren't you at dinner with the rest of us? Oh and what time was the argument?" Quentin asked.

"Well, really, I just needed a break after that. I decided to head to my room for some peace and quiet and was there when the sound happened. Did I really get peace and quiet? No! I couldn't stop thinking about what he said. It's why when I heard the sound, I didn't come running out because I thought it was probably like some celebration like fireworks or something, and I couldn't deal with that. Not then. Anyway, I think the argument was maybe around 6:00?," Rita replied.

"Great, that's it for now. If there is something else, I will let you know. You may go now," Quentin dismissed Rita.

***

Next was Aron in his trademarked Yale sweater.

"Hey, what up?" Aron asked.

"Uhh, I'm trying to solve a murder?" Quentin responded quizzically. "Oh yeah, sorry," Aron said.

"So why are you on this cruise? What's your story?" Quentin asked.

"Well, rumor was that Jason was on this cruise, right? So I was like whoa, Jason Spark is going to be here? This guy is a legend in the photo community, I mean he was so camera-shy, yet so successful. Like I didn't even know what he looked like till I saw him that first night. So I wanted to be the legend photographer who got a photo of Jason and an interview with Jason. More importantly, I had to make sure that Samantha didn't get the picture of him. You see, I had this sort of 'friendly' competition with Samantha since our college days. So there was no way I was passing up on this opportunity. And here I am. Also, my boss offered a very large bonus if I got an interview with Jason, which I drastically need right now."

"Okay, did you notice anything suspicious or out of the ordinary so far? Any ideas, really?" Quentin asked.

"Well, to be blunt, yeah. There was a lot of stuff going on.

This cruise is pretty sketchy, not gonna lie. I mean I saw Ash poking around Jason's room earlier. I saw Samantha running after Jason. In the middle, I think I saw Danny and Aldrich in deep conversation, which is weird anyway because I thought Aldrich couldn't carry a conversation with anybody. I even saw Hemant arguing with Jason, which was weird because I thought Hemant only argued with people in the gym about who can lift more. Oh yeah, the biggest thing, I saw Rita leaving from Jason's room's hallway right before dinner and she was mad. Like I'm talking furious. I was low-key scared of her. And then she didn't show up to dinner, either. That's who my bets are on, definitely Rita. I mean even if she didn't actually kill Jason, there was something definitely going on there," Aron replied.

"Interesting, so when was the last time you saw Jason?"

"Well, this had to be probably two hours before dinner, ish? So around 5:00 PM? He was being chased by Samantha; I distinctly remember that," Aron said.

"Okay, this was pretty informative. Thanks a lot, Aron. I will call you in if there's anything left," Quentin said and Aron left.

***

Next was Hemant's turn. In he walked with his usual dumbbells. *Let me guess, this guy was in the gym when the murder happened*, James thought.

"Please, take a seat. Tell us what happened that day," Quentin said.

"Well, as usual, I was at the gym. I mean, I love the gym," Hemant began. *Yeah, I can see that. Tell me something I don't know*, James thought.

"And then I was just at the gym. When I came out to get dinner, I found all this commotion around the body. I didn't even know it was Jason Spark till Ron told me. I'm actually quite disappointed, I was hoping to get Jason as a client. Oh well," Hemant finished dejectedly.

"Perfect. Now, what exactly do you do again? Why are you on the ship?" Quentin continued.

"I am an accountant. I handle the accounts of famous people and thus, was given tickets for this cruise to see if I can find some other big famous people such as the holy grail of all clients, Jason Spark," Hemant answered.

"Ok, so now I need you to remember everything that happened on this cruise, anything suspicious, anything at all, maybe even if it was something inconsequential, could be really important," Quentin said.

"Ok, so I got Ash to come here because of my extra tickets for this cruise. To be honest, I don't remember much because I was in the gym so much. Out of everybody, though, Rita, Danny and Aldrich all seem suspicious to me. I mean, Rita has been prowling all over the ship. Danny seems nervous all the time, especially since the murder. And Aldrich is on his own level, his pretentiousness alone makes him suspicious, but he also seems to hate Jason Spark with a passion so there's that, too. Come to think of it, I did see Aron and Aldrich also arguing one day in the dining room. But really, I don't know the people on here very well because I was too concerned with the gym and getting Jason Spark to be my client. Wish I could help more."

"Speaking about getting Jason Spark as your client, I heard that you two got into an argument before he died?"

"I wouldn't call it an argument. I was trying to give him my card to see if I could get him to use me as his accountant and he just rudely told me that I wasn't good enough for him and that I wasn't fit to be an accountant even for his servants. Now, I feel like I'm a decently good accountant, so that did upset me, so I got a little angry and might have said a few words. But I also calm down pretty quickly, so I disengaged from the situation and left. I don't really need him as an account, anyway. My life's pretty good as it is."

"Alright great. Thank you, this was very helpful," Quentin replied. Hemant then left. James could tell Quentin was getting excited in anticipation of solving this case, it was clear as day in his eyes. James was clueless, *I have no idea how the murderer got in, no idea how he got out, no idea why he would do it, and more importantly, why are three different people all confessing to a murder???*

***

Now it was Danny's turn. He walked in with his head held high, confidently. He then sat down and began, "So let's begin? I'm sure you're going to ask me where I was, my relation with Jason, etc. So let's cut to the chase, shall we? I was with all of you at dinner. I hadn't seen Jason since I first got on to the cruise. Remember, I even asked you about him? Mind you, this was all very sketchy indeed. It was like one of those 'Congratulations! You've won a cruise!' type of emails, which are almost always scams, but hey, this one worked out, ish. It was all rather quite good until the murder, of course. But yeah, that's pretty much my story, nothing too extensive."

"Anyone you find suspicious or anything weird at all?" Quentin asked.

"Actually, yeah, there was something. I think this was the night before the murder. I was taking my normal night walk and I saw Ash super drunk and arguing with Jason. I don't know about what. He also then went and attacked Jason. I don't know if that means anything, but I did notice that. That's the main thing that sticks out in my head," responded Danny.

Quentin's eyes lit up. He then asked, "So why did you stop working for Jason?"

"Well, creative differences, I suppose. I had this idea, he didn't like it. I left."

"Well, then why would he invite you onto this cruise?"

"No idea, that's kinda what I was wondering, too. I mean we didn't leave on the best of terms, so I was confused, but only a fool would pass up on a cruise like this," Danny replied.

"Well, I guess that's everything for now. Thanks again," Quentin said and dismissed Danny.

"Before I leave, one question, have you guys figured out how the killer got in the room?" Danny enquired.

"Not yet, but we're looking into it," Quentin replied.

"Well, I am somewhat well versed with technology. The doors seem to be electronically locked so if I were designing them, I would definitely create a master key that could unlock any of the doors for safety reasons. Of course, I would create a copy of the master key in case it was ever lost, but I wouldn't create any more copies for security purposes. It might be worth looking into," Danny stated.

"We'll look into it. Thanks," Quentin said and with that Danny got up and left the room.

***

Ron knocked and asked, "Can I come in?"

"Sure, come on in. Please take a seat," Quentin responded.

Ron came and sat down. "So tell me, what brings you here to this cruise?" Quentin asked.

"Well, I was basically asked by my boss to come here. You see, he really wanted this deal with Jason. And I couldn't really tell him no. So here I am. Although, I was really excited to see Fiji, never saw Fiji before. But I guess this murder kind of ruined the mood."

"What did you know about Jason Spark?"

"Nothing much, really. I knew he was a hugely successful business tycoon, but that was about it. I mean, his company is amazing; it is supposed to be one of the best places to work. Might make a better boss than my current one. Although then again, while I heard the benefits and salary and everything was awesome there, I've also heard that Jason himself is an extremely demanding boss and can rub people off the wrong away easily," Ron said.

"If you liked that company so much, why aren't you working there right now?"

"Well, I had applied. I got rejected though. Apparently, I wasn't 'innovative' enough," Ron responded.

"Oh, I'm sorry to hear that. Well, was there anybody who you think was suspicious or just anything happening on this cruise so far?"

"Not really. Everybody's pretty nice. Although I did see Samantha running after Jason maybe two hours before dinner? And then actually, if I remember correctly, I also saw Ash prowling around pretty soon after that near Jason's room. Oh and on my way to dinner, I saw Hemant going towards the gym and then I ran into Rita right before dinner. She looked really upset so I didn't actually end up talking to her. And then after that, I met you guys at dinner and here we are."

For someone who thought everyone's nice, this man just mentioned almost everybody on board except for us, James thought.

"So what was your day like today?" Quentin asked.

"Well, nothing much. I woke up kind of late. I then went to the gym to play basketball. I absolutely love basketball, it's my go-to sport for calming down. And then, I met you guys for dinner where I was talking to Danny who was pretty nice. He actually offered me a job, which was a big deal considering he was one of the main founders of Spark Industries. So that made my day. And then the grisly murder happened," he replied calmly.

This guy his one of the calmest people I've seen here. He needs calming down? Also what's this about Danny and founding Spark Industries, I thought that was solely Jason's company. We even just talked to Danny and he confirmed that they split, James wondered.

"I'm sorry, Danny was one of the main founders? He said he just used to work for Jason?" Quentin asked in surprise.

"Yeah, didn't you guys know? It's actually a huge legend in the computer science world. So Spark Industries is a brand new company and making huge waves. As usual, just like other major tech companies, there were two people who were involved. Danny was one. The other, of course, was Jason. Now Jason was known for his intelligence and shrewdness. He had already created algorithms to trade on the stock market and had amassed quite a fortune. Part of that fortune came through many, let's say, unethical ways. He possessed a lot of business acumen and was ruthless to boot. Also, rumor has it that Jason had a godfather in the business world who sheltered him and connected him with many opportunities. Someone who was a mogul in their own right. Jason invested almost all the money in Spark Industries, but Danny was the spokesperson. He pitched the ideas to many others purely in the computer science world. This got many people interested and they went to go work for the company. All was going well. Especially because they had some secret algorithm that allowed them to completely out-compete every other company. The algorithm was stored on Jason's home computers and completely detached from the internet, making it impossible to hack. And those computers never leave Jason's person. The moment that algorithm is leaked, well, that's the end of the company.

"Anyway, now the best part of the story. Right when the company was going to begin marketing to the public, Danny disappeared. Other employees became the spokespeople. Really, they were just Jason's puppets. Nobody knows why Danny disappeared. Rumor has it that Jason essentially framed him in some money laundering crime, which forced him to flee and allowed Jason to obtain full control over the company. Jason basically owned all 100% of the company's shares after this while Danny was left with nothing. It was actually very surprising to see Danny here and then find out he had been invited. I would imagine there was still a lot of bad blood between the two.

"But anyway, after that happened, rumors started flying about Jason's godfather disappearing, which allowed Jason to come into the limelight himself. Well, figuratively speaking, as nobody had still seen Jason's face until this week, really. That's a whole other mystery. Nobody knows why he's so reclusive. Some people think he's just shy. Some people think it's for a more nefarious purpose so that he can spy, which gives him a competitive edge. Some people think he doesn't even exist and that he's just a character made up, which is of course, ridiculous, given that we just saw him and there has been proof that he does exist such as a birth certificate. Me, I think he just does it to keep a semblance of mystery around him so that picks up sales," he answered with an air of mystery.

"Well, that is certainly useful. Also, you mentioned basketball is your go-to calming sport and you played it that morning. You're on vacation, why did you need to be calmed down?" Quentin continued.

Ron looked like he just kicked himself. "Well, you see, I thought I might as well get started with my work, so I asked Jason if I could have a meeting with him the day and he kicked me out of his room unceremoniously. Every time I saw him, I tried asking, and he just pointedly ignored me and kept walking away. Sometimes, he even ran away. So, naturally, I was getting angry with him because my job was on the line and he wasn't even bothered to listen to me."

"Ah I see. Now, I'm assuming your company is probably pretty big to try to get in a deal with Spark Industries. Why did they pick you for this job? Are you high ranking enough or?"

"Honestly, I'm not sure. I'm not that high ranking to have a 1-on-1 conference with the Jason Spark. Sometimes, I think my boss was just lazy and sent me or that maybe my calm demeanor might work. Especially because he tends to get angry and irritated pretty quickly. Other times, I think he wanted me to fail so that he could fire me. I'm pretty sure he's not a huge fan of me. Well, either way, if the latter was true, he got his wish now that Jason's dead."

"Ok, that should be everything. If there is anything else, we will let you know. Thanks!" Quentin concluded and Ron left.

***

Aldrich then sauntered in and sat down pompously, not even pausing to let Quentin say something. He began, "Make this brief. I have a business appointment soon that I must attend. I had no connection to Jason's untimely demise. I had another business appointment then and I was occupied with that phone call. I would tell you to ask them for confirmation, but that information is confidential. But regardless, there was no possibility of me being with Jason because I was preoccupied myself. Any other inquiries?"

"Well yeah. This is a murder investigation, I'm sure your 'business appointments' can wait. What's your connection with Jason? Why are you even here?" Quentin asked.

"Jason and I go way back. We were close friends a long time ago. That's it, nothing else. I also did not notice Jason after the first night's festivities," Aldrich answered.

"Ok well, if you were such close friends, why didn't you see him after the first night's festivities? Why did you even come here? Quentin continued to press.

"If you must know, we were estranged. A considerable amount of time had passed prior to this cruise where we neither spoke nor wrote to each other. Imagine my surprise at receiving a letter from him inviting me to this cruise. Then, I arrive and I find out he provided me with subpar accommodations. You can imagine my displeasure at this slight. So I did not wish to grace him with my presence and proceeded to enjoy the cruise without his company," Aldrich answered.

"So you're from England, correct?" Quentin asked, switching tactics. James looked at him with surprise in his eyes. *We never bothered them about where they're from. What's with this move?*

"England, yes, but more importantly, the nation of the United Kingdom of Great Britain and Northern —," Aldrich answered.

"Ireland, yes, we know. You see, I'm from there as well. I've never heard of your company. What exactly do you guys do?" Quentin interrupted.

"Well, we are an import-export business. It is not surprising you have not heard of us, we cater to the uber rich and wealthy. I'm afraid, as a result, we are relatively quiet on our publicity to preserve our sanctity," Aldrich responded without losing an ounce of his air of pomposity.

"You'll find me rather well-versed in companies and the workings of such companies, especially said import-export businesses. I think I can gather what I'm wondering, though. Let's move on. Did you see anything suspicious or out of the ordinary all cruise?" Quentin asked.

"Not exactly. Everything I saw felt perfectly ordinary to me, certainly not extraordinary. Would an argument suffice to be out of the ordinary?" Aldrich asked innocently.

"Yes, an argument would be out of the ordinary, who was it with?" Quentin replied, exasperation showing on his face.

"I did not want to say this as I do not interfere in other people's business, but I did see the argument between Jason and the girl who accosted me, I believe Rita was her name," he answered.

"What was the argument about?"

"I cannot be certain, but I believe Rita wished to speak with Jason about some normal economic theory and Jason did not wish to speak with a girl about economics, believing it to be a field not suited for women," Aldrich answered while leaning back in his chair. He looked quite satisfied in himself, almost more so than normal.

He feels like he won this interview. He knew he wanted to bring this up, but didn't want to bring it up unprompted, James realized.

"And what is your belief about that?" Quentin asked, eyes narrowing at Aldrich's body language.

"I certainly do not agree with Jason. I believe the field is suited for women, as I believe the field as a whole is a worthless endeavor," he answered.

He must be a delight in parties, I can't tell if he's worse than Jason or not, Jason thought.

"What a belief, impressive. You said Rita accosted you, when did that happen?" Quentin said, his voice level but his face betraying his anger and frustration at this man.

"Yesterday morning during breakfast."

"What happened exactly?"

"Well, I was enjoying breakfast. Toast, my classic favorite. And then Rita came to my table and asked if she could take a seat. Of course, I could not decline. In two and a half minutes precisely, she began to become incensed and directed the anger at yours truly. She picked up her coffee cup and spilled it on my three piece suit. It was Dolce Gabbana, a suit worth over ten thousand pounds, ruined beyond recognition. How can anyone do something so heinous?" Aldrich asked with self-pity glimmering in his eyes.

"Why did she get so angry?"

"I still do not know. We were speaking about her career and she had mentioned economics. I remember not even being mildly surprised at this as she looked perfectly suited for economics."

"Didn't you just say that economics is if I recall correctly, a worthless endeavor?"

"Well yes indeed, it is. And that is precisely what I told her. But of course, as a lady who is not married or an heiress, economics is perfect for her. It was a compliment as to her perfect understanding of her and her role in the world, at least until she is married and can focus on what is actually important."

"Which would be what?" Quentin said frostily.

"Ensuring her family is perfect and taking care of her family, of course," Aldrich replied looking sure of himself.

Quentin stared at him for a few seconds, unable to comprehend what Aldrich was saying. "So you're telling me that a woman's only role is to take care of her family which can only happen once she's married? And of course, before the marriage, she can do whatever she wants as long as it's a worthless endeavor such as economics?" He asked still struggling to understand Aldrich. James was stunned for a second and then was actively trying to restrain himself from murdering Aldrich in front of Quentin.

"Yes, that is correct. You are the first person to understand my beliefs. It must be because you and I share a home," Aldrich answered happily.

Now Quentin looked like he would likely be an accomplice to the murder of Aldrich. *It won't even be a murder, it would be a social service. For the good of mankind,* James thought.

"Look Aldrich, I'm surprised Rita spilled her coffee on you. You were lucky she was so controlled and exhibited such restraint. If I were her, I would probably beat you up in addition to spilling coffee, juice, throwing your toast at you, everything," Quentin said angrily.

"Oh my god. I cannot believe you spoke to me like that. Aldrich Appleton. I am Aldrich Appleton. Do you know who I am?" Aldrich stood up angrily.

"Yeah you just said your name twice," James commented.

"This is it. I cannot stand by such disrespect. If you have any other queries, do not bother to ask me. I must depart now," Aldrich said and then promptly departed the room.

James then said, "Well, at least he's gone. That's also everyone. What do you got, Quentin?"

5

"Alright, let's start from what we know. We know that Jason was murdered at 7:00 PM because that is when we were eating dinner and the body fell. We also know that during that time, Danny, Ron, Aron, Sarah, Samantha, Ash, you, and I were eating dinner. We know that Jason was killed by a single gunshot to the back. Where the gun is, we don't actually know yet for sure, we haven't found it. Next set of facts is in the crime scene. We know the computers were wiped clean. We know that there is a huge pool of blood in the middle of the room and the room overall is messy. We know that the room was locked from the inside. These are all the facts we know that shouldn't be subject to interpretation because there are no assumptions here, just plain cold facts," Quentin started.

He continued, "Now, let's look at our analysis without the interrogations first. We believe the killer was systematic, methodical, cold-blooded, and that this murder was premeditated. We believe that the computers could have been wiped for evidence or for corporate espionage. In the case of the former, our suspect pool is the exact same. But in the case of the latter, our subject pool narrows considerably as only a handful of people could have a motive to steal information, namely Ron, Danny, and Aldrich. Out of those three, Ron and Danny have solid alibis. Aldrich, let us say, does not. Now let's move on to what we got out of the interrogations.

"First up, the obvious main issue is the three confessions we have. Frankly, I don't think any of them did it, mainly because all three of them were with us at dinner. Now, why are they all confessing, I have no clue, yet. But first, I want to hear your opinions. Who do you think did it and why? What did you think of this?"

"Well, there was definitely no love lost between Jason and all the people on this cruise. Feels like almost everyone has a motive of some kind. I still don't think any of the three people who confessed did it, there has to be something else going on there. Also because what kind of idiot goes and confesses? I mean, you go to all that trouble and then just be like here I am, I did it? Doesn't make sense. A couple people all saw Rita leaving angrily from his room, and for that matter, I did, too. If I were a betting man, my money's on Rita, but also possibly Aldrich. Can you really get more suspicious than Aldrich, though? He left so angrily, for god's sake," James responded.

"You know, for once, I am actually quite happy with your thoughts. I think you're mostly right, especially about the three confessions. There's normally a couple reasons as to confessions: blackmail, overconfidence, or protection. There is always a chance one of them was blackmailed to confess, but all three of them? Seems unlikely. Now, maybe one of them really is the killer, and is just confident we won't get to him or her, so is confessing to throw us off their trail. This is always a possibility and is really common in those mystery books you keep reading. However, just because they were all with us at dinner, it is hard to believe. Plus, more importantly, that doesn't explain the other two confessions. Also, if you had paid attention to the interviews, you would have noticed that almost all three weren't nervous at all when they walked in, but became nervous when I asked them about the murder itself.

"Now, imagine you just killed someone, would you really come confess and not be nervous at all about the fact you just killed a man? Especially if it's 'guilt' eating at you, you should be trembling when coming in, not confident. And let's say maybe you're that overconfident killer, would you really start breaking down when asked about the murder you know every single detail about? Of course not, that should be your forte. This leaves me with the third option, protection. They somehow are all protecting the true killer and are taking the responsibility on their own shoulders so the killer can leave unharmed. Hence, why they are getting nervous about the details of the murder, because they wouldn't have done it and are worried about being caught in the act of lying. On top of that, remember all the questions I asked. None of them got the details right. They were purely guessing."

Quentin then paused, got a sip of water, and then continued, "What else do we know? We know that the last time anyone saw Jason was Rita at 6 PM. I'm inclined to believe her since Aron and Ash both confirmed that timeline. Danny, Ron, Aron, Ash, Samantha, and Sarah were with us at dinner, hence it is impossible that they did it. That leaves Rita, Aldrich, and Hemant. Now there are a couple key questions we have to answer before we get anywhere. First, what was Jason doing from 6-7 PM and how did the crime scene become so trashed? Second, how did the killer get in and out of the room? And third, why would those three be confessing even though they know they should have the perfect alibi? Once we can answer these questions, we should be able to identify motive and the killer. Let the game begin. But first, let's reexamine the crime scene."

***

Quentin walked back into the crime scene and

immediately yelled in exasperation, "the crime scene has been tampered with!!!!" James walked in and saw what he meant. The blood was wiped up, everything was back to normal, almost as if nothing had ever happened. James could see Quentin was furious. He was pacing back and forth, wringing his hands as if he wanted to strangle someone. He ran out and a few minutes later came back with the captain.

"Look at this monstrosity. Who came in here and cleaned this up? This was a murder scene, this is a murder investigation, we can't have crime scenes tampered with!" Quentin exclaimed.

"But, we didn't do this. I strictly told everyone to stay away. I don't know how this happened. Someone must have come in without us knowing," the captain responded.

"Well, we're back to square one, now, because you didn't know that someone came in" Quentin retorted. After seeing the captain's face, he relented, "I'm sorry, I'm just upset because we lost so much evidence. I know it's not your fault. I'll try to do what I can."

"If you need anything else, you know where to find me," the captain said and left without so much as a look back.

"What now, Quentin?" James asked.

"What now, indeed?" Quentin said while appearing lost in thought. He suddenly straightened up and said, "well let's see what we got. Maybe the killer left something when he was trying to clean up."

The room was immaculate. *Wow, this sounds exactly like Quentin's story the other night*, James thought.

Quentin noticed a wardrobe and immediately began rummaging through it. A few moments later, he took out something and after reading it, turned pale and looked at James. He pulled out a card from his pocket, nearly identical to the thing in his hand. *No, it was identical*, James noticed with a start.

Quentin had found a card saying *Catch me later*.

6

Quentin scoured the rest of the wardrobe and found a stack of cards, all identical to each other. All white with no designs, no logos, nothing. Except the three ominous words, *"Catch me later."*

The importance of this dawned on James,

Quentin walked back to the room in silence with the card and sat down, looking defeated for the first time ever. James came up to him and without even asking anything, Quentin began talking.

"It all makes sense. I'm blind and stupid not to have seen it before. Jonathan Ember, obviously it was a pseudonym. Jonathan Ember, Jason Spark, even a fool could have seen it, but I didn't. If I did, who knows, Jason probably would have been alive right now. Although, do I mourn his death, of course not. Jason was despicable. We've seen that on this cruise from all the interviews, remember? But he could have been in jail, but alive, and the killer wouldn't have blood on his hands. This was preventable, I could have prevented it, but I didn't because I was so stupid."

"But you couldn't have known. You tried your best," James responded.

"But what good did that do? Thing was it was obvious,

back then, the murder victim was Jason Spark's biggest rival. Jason had just started his business, but was close to being broke. The victim's company, Appleton Technologies, Inc, was the largest name in the field. He needed the victim out of the way, it was right there. After that day, Appleton Technologies became bankrupt and Jason began his ascent to a full-blown tech mogul. Of course, Appleton Technologies has now become Appleton Enterprises and are one of the last legitimate black market companies left eager to undercut Spark Industries. I know, 'legitimate black market' is an oxymoron. I don't know how else to describe it.

"Either way, the name similarities between Jonathan Ember and Jason Spark, too. It's so obvious. I even thought it might have been him, but I had no way to make sure because I had never seen Jason before. And when I heard Jason might be on this ship, I was going to finally see if he was Jonathan, but he wasn't. I had never seen Jason before. I even remember how Jonathan looked, I had interviewed him, but he had a weaker motive than the others so I dismissed him. But he was average height, white, but had a brown beard and was bald. Obviously, that was not Jason. Even if the beard was a disguise and he had shaved his head then, he couldn't have grown 8 inches in two years. It's impossible. The only thing I can think of is that Jason sent one of his men to do it. He had to. Or it's somehow not him and the killer planted the card knowing the story. But the card's identical to then, so the only way the killer could have planted it was if he somehow knew Jonathan. That's so unlikely and the coincidence with the name and motive too. It has to be Jason.

"But it's so disheartening, knowing I failed. Knowing I let a killer get away. Knowing it's my fault a man is dead and another man is a murderer. What type of detective am I? I keep saying I'm the world's greatest detective, but what use is that, if people keep dying? And I'm obviously not the world's greatest detective if I can't even solve crimes. I can't even solve this. I got everyone with an alibi saying they're guilty and everyone without an alibi saying they're innocent. All the physical evidence is gone. I don't know where the murder weapon is. I don't even know where the shell casing is. On top of all that, I have no idea how the murderer got in, got out, and disappeared before I got up there.

"Really, I know nothing. It's impossible. Everything is just against me. There, the crime scene was too clean. Here, the crime scene was too messy and now too clean. There, no one had alibis. Here, everyone has alibis. There, everyone was a suspect. Here, no one really is a suspect. That's the definition of a perfect crime then. This, is the definition of the impossible crime and I have nothing. Nothing at all," he said dejected.

James walked up to him and punched him in the chest. "Dude, get out of it. You solved so many crimes, remember those. Remember all the lives you did help. Remember the time you got someone off of death row, remember the time you saved an innocent man from going to jail, remember each of those times. Don't just focus on the one that got away, focus on the others that are in jail where they belong. Focus on the people you helped, not the one person you couldn't help. Imagine if you stopped working now, who's gonna solve this murder? Me? I can't even analyze one crime scene correctly. Think about who you're leaving the investigation to before quitting."

Quentin started laughing and said, "you're right, old friend. Although, you might be able to pull off the investigation, who knows? But yes, I can't give up now. Not while the killer is still out there. Maybe I couldn't help Jason, but I can at least make sure the killer doesn't get away to kill another day. Let's get out there and find this killer, somehow."

***

James was struck with an idea. He turned to Quentin and asked, "do we have security footage anywhere that we can look at the day of the murder?"

"That is an appropriate question James, I'm proud. There should be security footage, I doubt we'll get lucky and see the murderer, but who knows, let's go talk to the captain," Quentin replied.

Together, both of them wandered the halls until they found and entered the captain's quarters. Quentin began, "Captain, sorry about earlier, I was very distressed at losing my crime scene. Do you happen to have any security footage from that night?"

"As a matter of fact, I do. I'm surprised it took you this long to ask me about it, but I didn't want to step on your toes, all world's greatest detective and all," he replied scathingly.

Without losing a step, Quentin said, "great, can we see it? Specifically, the day of the murder from the morning outside Jason's room."

The captain pulled up the security footage and Quentin and James began to observe it. It showed Jason leaving the room around 12 PM and not coming back in until 5 PM when he was fighting with Samantha. At 1 PM, housekeeping came in and left with dirty sheets and towels. At 5:15, Jason came out again to talk with Ash until 5:20 PM when Ash left angrily. Then, around 5:30 PM, Jason left the room again. At 6:15 PM, he came back. At 6:30 PM, housekeeping came again and left with more dirty sheets and towels. At 7 PM exactly, Quentin was seen running up the stairs to break open the door.

"What? Where did Jason go?" Quentin asked.

"I'm not entirely sure," the captain responded.

"Go back and follow Jason after he left," Quentin ordered. The footage followed Jason wandering the halls until he saw

Rita where he briefly got into an intense conversation with which ended with Rita storming off around 6:00 PM. Then around 6:15 PM, he walked back into the hallway to go to his room.

"Can you go back to the footage of Jason's room around 1 and then skip to 6:30?" Quentin asked. After looking carefully at the footage, he exclaimed, "of course!"

Everyone looked at him and James could see his confusion reflected in the captain's eyes. "For the less detective-minded of us here, can you elucidate Quentin?" James asked.

"Certainly, it's the oldest trick in the book. The camera footage is a loop. It struck me as odd the very first time that housekeeping would come twice, but look carefully. It's the same dirty sheets and towels both times! Someone hacked into the database and looped the security footage."

"So what you're saying is that we don't know what happened from 6:30-7?" James asked.

"That is correct. Captain, when was housekeeping sent here?" Quentin asked.

"Let me check," he responded. After looking at the logs, he looked perplexed and said, "looks like housekeeping wasn't sent at all that day."

"Then the housekeeper must be our killer," James said happily.

"Maybe, but it doesn't make much sense. We know the murder happened at 7 PM and housekeeping came in at either 6:30 PM or 1 PM, neither time matches. Out of curiosity, can you see the previous day's footage?" Quentin asked.

"Certainly," the captain said.

After seeing the previous day's footage around the 1 PM mark, Quentin exclaimed, "look there, it's the same person again!"

"Well, then they can't be the killer after all," James said

dejectedly.

Quentin decided to go through the other footages of that night. He found Hemant as promised in the gym the entire time. He saw Ash, Sarah, Samantha, Ron, Aron, and Danny sitting in the dining room from 6:45 PM to 7:00 PM with Quentin and James. Aldrich walked in his room at 5 PM and didn't leave until the next day. Rita entered her room at 6:00 PM and walked out around 8:00 PM. Even the captain and the rest of the crew weren't spared, but they were all found in their spots the entire day.

Quentin looked surprised and said, "everyone has an alibi according to this. So there's only two possibilities. One, the killer snuck around without me realizing somehow or two, they were smart enough to loop the footage for not just Jason's room, but their room as well. But why loop it twice?"

7

The next day, Quentin was still deep in thought so James went to go see Samantha to see if he could clear any of the confusion up. Not about the time loop, he figured she didn't have the expertise to hack into the feed, but about the whole confessions. He found her on the top deck of the ship, sunbathing and on a FaceTime call. *Wow, this is a girl who just confessed to a cold-blooded murder and the first thing she thinks of doing is to go sunbathing?* James thought. He walked up to her and sat down and said, "Hey, what's up?"

Samantha ended her call and looked over to him and responded, "Hey, it's beautiful weather, isn't it?"

"Just one question. While it is indeed beautiful weather, you also confessed to a murder, is this really the first thing you think of doing?" James asked.

"Well, yeah, murder or no, got to enjoy the sunshine while it lasts, right? Oh also also, do you want to see a picture of my dog? He's so cute. My other dog's pretty annoying though."

James' heart melted. *How can I refuse to see a picture of a dog, what monster doesn't like dogs. Maybe the murderer, I guess.* "Yeah, of course, let's see this dog."

After spending about twenty minutes going through all of Samantha's pictures of her dog, James turned to Samantha and asked, "Why did you confess?"

Samantha looked slightly distressed and looked away for a split second and then turned to James. "I confessed because I did it, we went over this. Is this why you are here? Just to drill me on whether I actually did it because I actually did do it, ok? Please go away and stop bugging me about it." She then turned away and started shaking. After some time, James realized she was crying.

James didn't know what to do. *I wish I took the Emotional Support 101 class in college now.* "Hey, everything will be okay, I think. What's the matter? I can probably help. Actually, scratch that, maybe help," he said. *God, that class would be a lifesaver right now. Maybe help. What was I thinking? Even Quentin might be better than I am at actually helping, which is saying a lot. He normally can't help anyone on the other side of his monocle.*

"It's ok. I'm fine, it's just…idk what to do. You know what, James, you seem like a nice guy, so I'm going to tell you a little secret. Just please please don't tell Quentin; if you do, I will deny ever telling you anything. Ok? Promise?"

What am I getting myself into? James thought. "Of course, promise. What's the secret?"

"So…I didn't kill Jason. You know Ash right? Well, I saw him getting into that fight with Jason the day before where he bit Jason when drunk. And the next day when Jason died, I saw him pick something up from outside Jason's room, so I was almost certain that Ash did it. I confessed to protect him because I was the one who complained to Ash about Jason and I can't bear to see him get in trouble because of a problem I started. Everything else I said actually did happen, obviously except for the actual murder. Again, remember this is our little secret," Samantha said.

Then it hit James. All those times he saw Samantha and Ash together, the stories they both said while confessing, everything came together. "You love Ash, don't you? That's why you're blaming yourself for his actions," he said.

"Well, duh, I thought that was pretty obvious. Now I can see why Quentin is the detective around here," she responded.

Now I wish I had taken Relationships 101 in college. So many classes that would have been helpful and what do I take? Orgo, James thought.

"Ok, well, does Ash know about this?" James asked.

"Of course not, and if you tell him…" she threatened while giving him a smile.

Those are the worst kind of threats, the threats they give while smiling. James responded, "Ok, ok, I won't tell him. Although, just putting this out there. Why would you automatically assume Ash did it? Some faith you have in him. Just saying, most people think the person they love can do no wrong. Here you are thinking he has the ability to murder someone?"

"Well, I thought it would be an accident or something. Definitely not a cold-blooded murder. I don't think Ash is capable of that. I thought maybe he might have fought with Jason, which resulted in him killing Jason. That's it," she responded.

"Hmm ok, makes sense, I guess. Anyway, I'll head out now, enjoy your sunbathing and your dog," James said as he turned and left, trying to find the next suspect.

***

After searching the entire boat, James found Ash pacing in a secluded nook on the fourth floor. Ash was muttering to himself constantly. "Hey Ash, is everything ok?" asked James.

Ash turned and had a brief look of panic before he relaxed. "Yeah, everything's fine. How are you, James?" he asked.

"Everything's good. The investigation is going on fine. Although this is ghastly business, isn't it? Really can't believe such a nice cruise is tarnished by a murder," James replied.

Ash begins to contemplate life and after an eternity, begins to speak, "So why are you here? You obviously aren't here to talk about the weather."

Wow, straight to the point, no beating around the bush with this guy, James thought. "Ok, you got me. I'm here to ask you for real. Why did you confess to the murder?"

"Well…I thought it was pretty obvious. I confessed to the murder because I killed Jason, there's no two ways about it. If that's all, I'll be on my way, then," Ash said.

"No, that's not all. Look, I'm not stupid. You were with us during dinner, you have the perfect alibi. You also wouldn't be this distressed right now if you were truly guilty and had already gotten that burden off your chest. Who are you covering for and why?"

"Wow, you would make a pretty good psychiatrist, trying to read me like that. However, you're wrong, I have nothing to tell you, at all," said Ash. He then turned and began to walk down the hall towards the staircase.

"You're doing this for Samantha, aren't you?" James yelled down the hall.

Ash stopped, and then slowly turned around. *Does he do everything in slow motion?* James thought. "What did you say?" Ash asked.

"You're doing this for Samantha, aren't you?" James repeated. Ash walked closer and asked, "What did you say?"

"You're doing…am I speaking in Spanish? 'What did you say? What did you say?' You know very well what I said," James said. "You love Samantha and are doing this for her."

Ash sat down in a chair, shoulders slumped in defeat. "How did you know?" he asked.

"Well, it was quite simple, really. I've noticed the way you face her, the slight change in your angle, the change in your posture, as if you are trying to look more manly and handsome. Every time you talk to her, your voice drops a couple notes. Actually no, I'm not that observant; I need a monocle for that. I just guessed, but now I know," James said triumphantly.

Ash's shoulders slumped even more. "Well, don't tell anyone, ok? I don't want her feeling guilty that I'm going to jail for her."

"You're not going to jail, not for her, not for anyone. We're going to find the real killer. Also why do you think she did it then?"

"I saw her getting into an argument, remember? I thought she was the only one with motive."

"Well you're really some lover if you have that much faith in her that you think she killed someone."

"Wow, I never thought of it like that. So you think she's innocent?"

"I do, I don't think she had it in her to murder someone like that so you shouldn't need to worry and you definitely don't need to put the blame on you just on the off chance she did. That's just incredibly stupid."

"Thanks James, you really helped me out here. Can you please tell Quentin what I said, that I didn't do it?"

"Of course Ash, no problem. Either way, I must be going, more suspects to interrogate," James said while turning around and exiting the hall.

***

James was walking along the sixth floor when he found Sarah eating a snack on the promenade. *Ah, finally, the third suspect, let's see who she loves, now shall we?* James thought. "Hey Sarah, what's up?" James called.

Sarah finished her snack and said, "Hey James, nothing much. Just eating. What about you? Convinced I did it, yet? I don't know if you can tell, but there is quite an air of tension on the ship, tight enough that just one little tear could bring down the whole ship, and it's all because you haven't decided who the murderer is, even though I came up to you and said I did it. I never intended to harm the rest of the ship, yet that is what's happening right now, and I hate it, all because you guys are scared of believing me?"

James didn't know what to say. After a few seconds, he regained the use of his tongue and said, "No. I don't believe you, not for one bit. You were there with us when the attack happened. I think you're covering for someone. Someone you just met. Someone you think or know committed the crime. Wait, you're in love with someone. Is it Ash?"

Sarah's face had a momentary look of panic. "How did… wait what are you talking about? I…I told you I…I did it," she sputtered. *Like a deer caught in headlights*, James thought. "It is Ash," he said.

Sarah's shoulders slumped in defeat. "You got me. Yeah, I'm in love with Ash. After what happened last time, I couldn't let anything happen to Ash, this time."

"What happened last time?" James asked.

"Well, there was this guy, a few years ago. I loved him and I thought he loved me, too. After many years of dating, we decided to marry. My parents were super against it because they all thought this man was a cheat, but I didn't listen to anything they said. I went to the altar and I got a call saying he was on his fishing trip and his ship capsized. He had drowned. This was over five years ago and I still remember that day as vividly as ever. I had all my dreams for the future crushed, my world turned upside down. I used to have so much confidence, so much drive, but then, I had no idea what I was supposed to do.

"I moved back home, to be close to my parents and continue my life. But, I had to push myself really hard to get back on track. I was told that a lot of people had the same situation I did, but they were able to pick themselves up and move on. I just didn't know how I was supposed to do it. I was beyond devastated and broken; I was ready to just give up. I even did give up. I wandered everywhere, my life a shadow of what it used to be." Sarah said and then started crying.

"Same situation? But how, this can't have been a common occurrence," James said incredulously.

"You know what I mean, similar situations with the love of their life leaving them. I can't believe that's what you're focusing on. What made it even worse was the moment I saw Jason, he reminded me so much of him that I started thinking about him and had started crying. Then, Ash walked over to me and talked to me and got me out of it. I was in such a vulnerable place and Ash helped me so much," she replied as she continued crying.

James began to curse his college education and course selection once again and tried to comfort her.

Sarah then stopped crying momentarily and explained, "this is why I needed to make sure Ash doesn't go to jail. It took me this long to actually find someone else that I think I can be happy with, I needed to make sure I don't lose him too."

Sarah then resumed crying and ran away from the hall. James looked up at the roof, *Why am I so bad at this?*

***

James burst into Quentin's room, excited to share what he found. He found Quentin meditating in his chair, eyes closed with the monocle put to the side, his blue hair laying flat. Without opening his eyes, Quentin goes, "Leave the food here on the table. Thank you so much." When he didn't hear a reply, he cracks open one eye and sees James. "My apologies, James. I thought you were the room service person. I'm actually quite ashamed. Please have a seat," he said while gesturing to an open chair.

James sat down and said excitedly, "You wouldn't believe

what I found out. I talked to Sarah, Samantha, and Ash. It's a whole love triangle. Both Sarah and Samantha love Ash and thought he did the crime so confessed, and Ash loves Samantha so he confessed when he heard that she had confessed. In other words, none of them did it! Plus I even did some Quentin-y analysis. Samantha is too empathetic; she cared about her dog so much, there's no way she can be this cold-blooded murderer. Ash was way too distressed even though he had confessed, almost like he was having second thoughts about confessing. And Sarah literally got up and started crying. Now you tell me, what kind of murderer does that?" James ended on a triumphant note as if he had solved the entire mystery.

Quentin just seemed bored. "That's it? Boring. We already knew that they didn't do it. I'm sure you tried your best, though. Let's get to the interesting stuff, then? What were your actual conversations with them? More than just that they're innocent."

Wow, the thanks I get from helping. I guess consulting isn't the move for me. Should have never given up computer science in college. What did I even do in college? Oh yeah, finance and 'consulting'. Could have done prelaw, premed, emotional support, but noooo, had to do finance. Waste of time, James thought.

Quentin coughed, "Umm James, actual conversations?"

James snapped to attention and said, "Oh yeah. Well, with Samantha, we talked about her dog for a while and how she loved Ash. With Ash, we talked about how he loved Samantha and he was scared of her finding out. And with Sarah, she mentioned how her ex-boyfriend drowned in a fishing accident right before their wedding."

"Hmm—" Quentin was saying when he was interrupted by a knocking on the door. "Who's that?" Quentin asked. James got up to open the door and saw Aron. Aron looked frightened and started saying, "Ok, I have something really important to tell you. I was silent this long because I was scared for my life, but I need to tell you guys now. It was—"

8

Aron fell forward in mid-sentence. There was a bullet wound in his back. Quentin and James jumped up and ran towards the door. There was nobody. Completely empty. With the commotion, Sarah came out of her room, all disgruntled. Her eyes were deep red and puffy. It appeared as if she had been crying for the past hour.

"What happened?" Sarah asked while sniffling. Then she saw Aron's body lying in the doorway and shrieked. The entire cruise ship shook and immediately Ash came out of his room with a look of panic in his eyes. Rita ran out, looking ready to fight a dragon. Hemant rounded the corner with a dumbbell in each hand, as usual. Samantha came up the stairs with her camera. Ron came down the stairs with a basketball in hand, as if he had just beaten Michael Jordan in pick-up basketball. Danny came, looking nervous as always. Even Aldrich appeared, dabbing his mouth with a napkin very ungentlemanly.

"What was that ghastly noise?" Aldrich asked calmly. He then saw the corpse and exclaimed, "Oh my! Golly, what is happening?"

"Why don't you say gosh and gee with that too while you're at it?" Ash asked. He was obviously in a bad mood. "A man died and you're sitting here, exclaiming 'Oh, my!' As if this is some kind of show and Aron's going to get up any minute from now and be like 'Hey guys! What did I miss, want a picture?' Can't you see how some people are being affected by this?" Ash let out all his steam and began to look at Samantha, who had started crying in the corner.

"Hey guys, just calm down. No need to get so riled up," Ron said.

"What do you mean, calm down? This guy just got shot in the back and you're telling me to calm down? Quentin, this is all your fault. What type of detective are you? Can't even find the murderer. What if it's me or Hemant or Samantha next? What good are you? Sitting there with a monocle, thinking you're better than all of us. I've seen your work in action. You haven't done anything. Aron died literally in front of you trying to talk to you and you couldn't even help him. How can you help all of us?" Ash exclaimed.

"How did you know Aron died in front of us?" Quentin asked quietly and the whole room became dead silent.

"I...I...." Ash stuttered and then became silent.

After a brief awkward silence, Samantha looked at him and moved slightly away and said, "I can't believe you did this, Ash. What monster are you? First killed Jason and then killed Aron. Stay away from me." After giving this short monologue, before waiting for an answer, she ran down the stairs and out of sight.

Ash went through a rainbow of emotions from disbelief to anger to sadness. He turned to Quentin and James and said, "I'll tell you what I know. It's not much, but maybe it can help."

***

Ash walked into their room. *He looked unsettled, as if someone just accused him of murder*, James thought. *Oh wait, the whole cruise just did. I don't know if he did it, though. You would think he would be a little bit smarter than that. I don't know what Quentin's thinking either, he always holds his cards close to his chest. Guess I'll find out soon enough. I remember this old mystery Quentin solved about a train, wait no, an airplane, I think. Quite close to this. He solved it just sitting on the sofa. Although I sincerely believe this case is considerably harder, I don't think I've ever seen Quentin this agitated yet about a case. And if Ash truly did it, he proved to be the stupidest murderer we've seen. Everyone saw him around the room, everyone saw him get into the fight with Jason, he confessed to it earlier, and now let slip a detail about Aron's murder. That's like four strikes, he should have been out a long time ago.*

Ash found a chair and sat down, looking over his shoulder to ensure no one followed him. He sighed and began explaining his story, "Alright guys, I wasn't clear with you from the start. The truth is as I told James, I didn't do anything. I only confessed to save Samantha —"

"Yes, yes, James told me. I still am loathe to believe you because that just sounds so stupid. You had no reason to suspect that she did it," Quentin interrupted.

"Actually, that's not quite true. You see, the day Jason died, I saw her getting into an argument with Jason right before dinner around 5. Then, the thing I picked up, that wasn't a pin. It was an SD card, the exact kind Samantha had. Along with that, the next day, I overheard Samantha talking to Aron saying that she knew Aron saw her arguing with Jason at 5 and that she knew how it looked. The thing was, she didn't even sound confident when she told Aron she didn't do it. And then I overheard her practicing a confession! At that point, everything lined up and I knew it had to be her so I came to you confessing."

"But you had to know that Samantha was with us at dinner so it couldn't be her."

"Oh yeah, I forgot about that," Ash looked genuinely confused.

Quentin let out an exasperated sigh and said, "alright, so you couldn't have come in here to just tell us that you confessed to save Samantha. What about Aron?"

"Right, well after I talked to James, explaining him the situation, I realized that Samantha couldn't have done it. I then decided to do some investigating myself. I remembered Aron and Aldrich getting into it earlier in the week, so I went to go pay Aron a visit to see what that was all about. When I went to go talk to him, he said he made a huge mistake and hid something and was just going to tell you all about it. I was shocked honestly and he left to go talk to you. I then remembered why I was there in the first place, to talk to him about Aldrich. I followed him out into the hall where I saw him falling down after being shot. I knew you would be looking at me, so I ran back into the room and waited a little bit before coming back out."

"Did you happen to then see the shooter?"

"I couldn't, I was too scared of being caught."

"Well, that's some story. You come up with this random other shooter who you conveniently didn't see," Quentin responded.

"Please, you have to believe me, I actually had nothing to do with either murder."

"Well if we believed everyone who said that, we would catch no murderer ever. Also, I heard you got drunk and attacked Jason one night. Is that true?"

Ash hung his head. "I'm not entirely sure, I do think it is true. He was just really acting up, especially around Samantha and Sarah and I was fed up of it. He just felt like such a bad person that I did get into it with him one night. I didn't mean to attack him, though."

"Is that how he got his bruise on his arm?"

"I didn't know he had a bruise, but I would imagine that it was. I might have…accidentally bit him."

Quentin nodded as if that made sense to him. "Sure, that's a sign of an innocent person."

"Please, I know I got angry, but I didn't kill him."

"How hard can it be that the night he died, you also 'got angry' and killed him. I'm sorry, anger is normally not a justified reason. I get why you would hate him. By all accounts, he was a deplorable person, but that doesn't excuse killing him."

"I didn't kill him!" Ash yelled.

Quentin stood up and began pacing around the room, muttering to himself, completely lost in thought. After ten minutes, Ash looked nervously around and asked, "can I leave now?"

Quentin looked startled, "oh I didn't realize you're still here. Go, I don't need you anymore."

Ash got up and left nervously. James kept looking at Quentin acting like a real madman. He was walking around the room constantly talking to himself. Eventually, he sat down, looking completely unsatisfied. He said, "it's late James. You should go get dinner if you haven't yet. I have to go check on something with the captain about the access to the rooms."

James made sure Quentin would be good without him and headed down to the dining hall. There, he got his food and sat down and observed the tense atmosphere. Ash had gotten food and was going to sit next to Samantha, but she turned away from him and left him alone at the table to go sit with Sarah. *Poor guy, rejected by the one who he sacrificed so much to save in his mind*, James thought. Hemant was talking to Aldrich, giving him his card. Rita was also eating alone. Ron and Danny were in the corner, talking furiously, and James could hear words like "machine learning," "AI," "algorithm." *Half the ship looks like nothing has happened while the other half looks like they can't trust anyone on the ship. What should we even do?*

James then observed Rita getting up and walking over to his table. "Hey, can I sit here and eat with you? I'm getting a bit scared and the atmosphere here just isn't welcoming. You're one of the only people here who seems like a genuinely nice person."

"Sure, of course," James replied and Rita sat down and began eating. "So, I don't mean to pry, but how's the investigation going?" Rita asked.

"Well, you know, it's going. I can't say too much because I don't want to disclose too many details," James answered.

"Oh right, of course. I'm guessing I'm a big suspect?"

"Everyone's a suspect, at least according to Quentin."

"And according to you?"

"Well, there's probably a few people I think are more likely to be the killer than not. For instance, Aldrich has been so weird this entire cruise. And no offense, but the only three people who don't have an ironclad alibi are Aldrich, Hemant, and well, you. But I'm 70% sure it's Aldrich."

"And the other 30%?"

"20% you and 10% Hemant, only because you lied to us about your argument with Quentin," James stated. *I don't care if I offend her. Maybe, I can scare her into telling the truth just like Quentin did with Ash.*

"I can understand that. I didn't want to lie, not really, but I knew how it looked. I watched enough mystery movies and shows. I mean when is it really not the person who just had an argument minutes to hours before the person died and is probably one of the last people to see the victim? I get why maybe some mystery shows don't do it because it doesn't sell, but still. So I couldn't admit it, until I guess you must have heard me," Rita replied.

"Well, yeah I did hear you. I didn't think too much about it until the body dropped, which had to be awful timing if you really didn't kill him. But still, you had to believe that Quentin would figure something out."

"I guess I did. I just panicked. I'm sorry," Rita said while slowly picking at her food. *Well, I guess Quentin's tactic didn't work, but I think she might be telling the truth.*

"But do you think Ash really killed Aron?" Rita asked.

"We're not sure, yet. He could have, but the timing is really special. So we're still looking into it," replied James. *I need to make sure I don't give away too much information.* James looked around, Sarah and Samantha were eating in silence. Danny and Ron had also stopped talking. Hemant was continuing on as normal, but Aldrich looked listless.

They're all paying attention to the conversation between Rita and me, they want to see if I give up any information! James realized.

"So when do you think you'll find the killer?" Rita asked pressing for information.

"Well, hopefully soon, so we can enjoy the rest of the cruise, if there's something to enjoy," James replied darkly. "Anyway, I should get going. I think Quentin needs me. If I find out anything, I'll let you know. And the rest of you as well," James continued. Everyone in the room immediately turned away to look at their food and began talking about the weather. James got up and left the room to check on Quentin. *We need to solve this murder soon!*

9

James began walking back to his room and soon ran into Quentin running from the captain's room.

"Whoa Quentin, what are you up to now?" James asked.

"No time, have to try a theory out. I talked to the captain and he said there were some all access cards made, one for himself and one for Jason. Do you remember seeing such a card in Jason's room?"

"Honestly, I'm not sure. It's been so long and it was so messy," James responded.

"I'll answer that for you, there wasn't such a card. This answers how the killer got in the room afterwards to clean it!" Quentin exclaimed.

James was still perplexed but followed Quentin into Jason's room. "You go inside and lock the door, but don't bolt it." Quentin ordered.

James went into the room, locked the door, and was taken aback at the sight of the room. "Quentin, I think you might want to come see this," he called out. Quentin tried to enter the room, but the lock didn't budge. James opened the door for him and Quentin exploded into the room with a look of surprise etched on his face.

The high-tech batcave-esque room was gone. All the

computers had vanished and it looked like just another random room on the cruise ship. "Are you sure we're in the right room?" James wondered.

"This is definitely the room, someone must have taken all the computers," Quentin responded and immediately ran out again.

This guy will make me run a marathon around the ship soon enough, James thought irritably and chased after him. Quentin had burst into the captain's room and was angrily questioning the captain.

"What happened to the room? This is the second time it's been tampered with. What kind of operation are you guys running here? Also, not to mention, the key you gave me didn't even work!" Quentin exclaimed.

"I'm sorry, I don't know what you are talking about. None of my people have gone into the room since the murder. That key definitely works, I've checked it myself earlier. And this is my key. As I mentioned earlier, there's only one other copy and that was with Jason. This key has to work. Which room did you try it on?"

"Jason's room. We locked it and tried the key; the door didn't budge."

"Are you sure it wasn't bolted?"

"Positive."

"Let me check something," said the captain as he went to his computer to check the logs. He came back, puzzled.

"Looks like someone hacked into the database and changed the access codes for Jason's room. This was the day of Jason's murder, right around 12 PM. They removed the master key code and added another code. Then, the next day, the second code was removed. So currently, the only code for Jason's room is Jason's card."

"I have Jason's card, though. So I know no one has that. Then how did they get in the room?" Quentin wondered.

"Can you tell which card was added that day?" James asked.

"Sure, that card belongs to…Aron" the captain replied.

After a minute of stunned silence, James spoke up, "well, that's useful. Aron's dead. There's no way he was the killer so what was even the point of adding his code? More importantly, how did the killer enter then?"

"That is the question, isn't it? This case just feels like dead end after dead end. There's a lot of evidence, but none of it matches up with each other. I feel like everyone is both telling the truth and lying. It truly is such a weird case," Quentin said and began walking out the door.

"Thanks captain," said James hastily and followed Quentin out the door.

"You said everyone's at dinner right?" Quentin enquired.

"Yeah, everyone I can remember at least," James answered.

"Great, then time to break and enter," Quentin stated.

James was stunned, but continued to follow Quentin.

***

Quentin stopped in front of Ash's room and took out the master card to swipe into his room. James looked around uncomfortably and followed Quentin into the room. "Uh Quentin, isn't this breaking and entering and therefore illegal?" James asked.

"Yes, this is the definition of breaking and entering. That's why I said a few minutes ago, 'Time to break and enter'," Quentin responded and began searching the room.

The room was relatively sparse, nowhere near as nice as Jason's room or even James' room. There was a queen size bed in the middle with the sheets bundled in one corner of the bed. *Ash must have gotten in a lot of trouble as a kid for not making his bed*, James thought. His bathroom had the cruise toiletries on a stand. His one suitcase was opened, its contents spread out all over the floor and room as a whole. *I guess we can search through everything and he won't even know,* James thought. Quentin immediately began rifling through the suitcase and the assortment of clothes spread around the room like a Turkish bazaar.

"A shirt, another polo shirt, jeans, cargo shorts one, cargo shorts two, cargo shorts three, I don't think we're getting much here," James observed.

"What an astute observation James, are you sure you don't want to be the detective?" Quentin asked sarcastically without so much as a look at James while continuing to throw clothes over the room.

"You don't actually think it's Ash, do you?" James asked.

"You mean after I grilled him? No, I don't. For one, he was with us at dinner. Two, while he seems like a very intelligent and methodical man, he doesn't seem like a killer when he's that careful. He does get angry like he was saying, but that doesn't fit the crime at all. He's not a cold blooded killer, for sure," Quentin replied.

"Then why did you bother him so much, the poor guy?"

"Well, I needed to make sure and more importantly, I needed to find an explanation for the bruise and the only way I could do that was scare him into telling me the truth for once."

Poor guy, if he just said the truth earlier, he wouldn't be in this mess where no one wants to even talk to him, thinking he's the murderer. On top of that, he thinks Quentin still thinks he did it. James shook his head and continued observing Quentin scouring the room.

After ten more minutes of searching, even Quentin admitted defeat and started trying to rearrange the clothes into an ordered chaos state. "I give up, how does he manage to find anything here? Either way, I don't think he will think his room was broken into. Let's get going," Quentin said and promptly exited the room.

***

The next room was Samantha's. It was even more sparse than Ash's room in terms of the cruise-provided amenities. Her room was full of camera equipment and her one suitcase in the corner. Quentin rummaged through her drawers and wardrobe and found it all to be empty. It was as if she never even unpacked her stuff or came with very little stuff.

Imagine the news title when we get back. Samantha now has full reign now that Aron is out of the picture. Ha, picture, James said chuckling to himself.

Quentin noticed it and raised his non-monocle eyebrow and then continued searching. After a few minutes, even he gave up and looked at James with resignation in his eyes. "Well, this was a bust. Two rooms with nothing so far," Quentin said.

"Hey Quentin, remember when we met Samantha. Did she really strike you as someone who came here actually planning a murder?" James asked.

"Honestly, not really. She really did seem like she wanted to get a picture with Jason. She seemed at least sincere then. Although I can understand her wanting to kill Jason when he was so uptight and cruel later, however. Although…" Quentin trailed off. James could see the wheels turning in his head.

"If she didn't plan it in advance and if she did it, where would she have gotten the gun?" Quentin wondered.

"That's what I was thinking. Remember, we went through security on the way in. I can't imagine someone smuggling a gun in and not getting caught," James replied.

"Honestly, I'm not sure how someone would be able to bring a gun in. It is perplexing," Quentin responded and looked lost in thought.

He spends so much time lost in thought that I don't know what to do. *Should I interrupt him? Should I let it play out? Is it like sleepwalking where you shouldn't wake them up? Is that even right? I wonder if he thinks like this, too. Do I look lost in thought right now? I guess I am. What do you know? Lost in thought about being lost in thought. Look at me go. So meta*, James kept thinking and staring into space.

"Hey James, we should probably get going," Quentin said interrupting James' circular thoughts.

Wow, how the tables have turned with Quentin snapping me out of thought, thought James as they left the room, hopefully leaving no trace.

***

Quentin and James then entered Ron's room. It was completely empty. There was a backpack in the corner with a few clothes and nothing else anywhere other than the standard bed that was perfectly made.

What is this? Ash should see this and talk to him. Maybe pick up some tips, James thought.

Quentin emptied the backpack on the bed and there was just one suit and a pair of shorts and t-shirts, all wrinkled beyond repair. *Well, this is pretty anti-climactic. We're 0 for 3 so far. Also wasn't he here to get a deal with Jason? I guess that explains the suit, but still. Is he a high-ranking individual or not? If he is, you would think he would at least have a better suit or more than a backpack. If he's not, why would Jason even talk to him? Let's see what Quentin has to say about it,* James wondered.

"Hey Quentin, Ron said he came here for a deal, right? Well what's with just a backpack and that too with a wrinkled suit?" James asked.

"If I had to guess, I don't think Ron was lying. He did come here for a deal. Except, I don't think he was too keen on the deal. I think he was just listening to his boss. Notice when he explained why he was here, his eyes betrayed boredom.

He didn't particularly want to be here, but it sounded like he had to. That would explain the lackluster effort. Not to mention, Jason is a tech mogul. I don't think he's one to care about appearances. I mean he was wandering around in a t-shirt and shorts for most of the cruise as well. On top of all of that, Ron already was rejected from Jason's company, so maybe he came here for a job offer instead. Either way, I don't believe he came here with a nefarious purpose," Quentin answered.

He was talking to Danny very intently and Danny did say he used to work with Jason. Maybe Quentin has a point with the looking for a job offer, James thought.

One thing I never asked Quentin. Why are we here? He just called me one day saying here's a ticket, but why is he here? Who invited him? We're wondering about everybody else. Maybe there's a clue in why we're here? James kept thinking.

"Quentin, another question. Why are you here? Who gave you your ticket?" James asked promptly.

"I'm surprised it took you this long to ask me. When I offered you the ticket, you jumped on it without even asking why. I thought I had rubbed off on you more. Every action has a reason and it's important to find the reason even if it is not important. Finding explanations for everything can either rule something out or put something under a more focused spotlight. Maybe an explanation can lead to even more questions. Oh well, better late than never—"

"Quentin, I'm sorry I'm taking longer to learn, but can we get to the answer quickly please?" James interrupted impatiently.

"Oh yes. You see, I had checked my mail one day and got an envelope with two tickets to a cruise, receipt of a million dollars transfer from an offshore account, and a typed letter saying that there would be a crime here and my services would be helpful. I wasn't sure what the crime was going to be, but I really hoped it wasn't a murder. Something like a robbery would be significantly better. So I decided to come here anyway. If nothing else, maybe I can help someone out. Imagine my shock at the murder and you can see why I reacted so strongly to the card reminding me of the unsolved case. I had another chance at saving a life, I had the information in front of me, and I still couldn't. Either way, with that information, if someone planned a murder that far in advance, we have a much clearer picture of psychologically who the murderer could be. Someone with not only a huge level of planning, but someone who is willing to taunt a detective, not only inviting them to the scene of a murder in advance, but paying them to be there just to play a game with them. We're playing with a much more dangerous adversary than I have ever seen before." On that ominous note, Quentin left the room with James hurrying to follow him.

***

They then entered into Danny's room. Danny's room was completely empty. It looked almost as if no one lived there. Surprisingly, to bed was still made, the bathroom was just a way it was when James had first moved into his room, and even the TV was set to its factory settings. James thought to himself, *Wow this guy must be extra clean. There's nothing here. Not even Quentin would find something here.*

Quentin was not one to be discouraged however. He began rummaging around the drawers and the wardrobe. He picked up random things in the drawers and started muttering to himself like he usually does. James began to wonder what exactly goes through Quentin's mind on a daily basis. *How does he see things in random pieces of clothes that looks like they weren't worn once. I wonder where he gets his try cleaning done I need to ask him for their number. This is a whole new level,* James wondered.

Quentin continued trying to find under pieces of evidence in the room, but then soon sat down the bed and gave up. *Wow that is probably the first crease the bed has seen since you often*, James thought.

"How does he actually do this?" James asked.

"I wonder, too. I've never seen such a room. It's in very stark contrast to Ash's room. Maybe he should pick up a few lessons," Quentin replied. "Anyway, let's continue on to the next room. I don't think there's much to gain from here."

***

Next up, Sarah's room. Sarah's room was very meticulously organized come. All of her clothes were neatly piled up in the wardrobe. Her bed was carefully made. Even the bathroom was well-organized. It wasn't like Danny's room where it looks like no one lived there, but it was still a lot cleaner that most of the other rooms in the beginning. Quentin looked absolutely delighted in such a room.

I think it has to do with Quentin's need for meticulousness. He absolutely despise the first couple rooms because of how messy they were. Maybe he also sees something about the killer based on how the room is organized. Didn't he say something about how the killer would have premeditated everything? Maybe that is why he's delighted. I wish he just told me what he sees in a room. He's always in a rush to just get out and move on. Oh well, I guess that's how he works, James thought.

Quentin, as per usual, began to first go to the wardrobe and then the subsequent drawers. He checked each of the drawers in the wardrobe and found nothing of use. He then began to look in the cabinets in the bathroom. After a few minutes, he started taking out items in the bathroom, yet still found nothing. He put back each of the items to make sure it looked like no one had entered the bathroom and continue to search the rest of the room. He then found a vase that was sitting in the corner of the bathroom. He opened it and looked inside and a look of surprise and then victory dawned upon his face.

What could it be? It has to be vitally important doesn't it, James wondered. "Quentin, what is it? I'm dying to know. Is it important?" James asked.

"You could say that," Question answered. He then began taking out whatever was inside the vase very slowly. *He always loved to be a showman, didn't he,* James thought.

After 20 seconds of Quentin looking at James, trying to see his reaction, he took out whatever was inside the vase. It was…a gun.

"Quentin, is that the murder weapon?" James asked.

"It certainly looks that way. There's two bullets missing, which would match with what we know about the two murders. I just wonder though…" Quentin trailed off.

"What? What do you wonder? What am I missing?" James asked relentlessly.

"Well, Sarah was with us during dinner. And even if she somehow did kill Aron, why would she keep the murder weapon with her? That just sounds like awfully poor planning, which given the state of the room, doesn't really match her character."

"Well, it was in a vase in the corner of the bathroom. I mean I don't think she thought someone was going to come and check her room while she was out at dinner, let alone so carefully like what we're doing. This is illegal, remember?"

"Even then, why hold on to it? We're on a cruise ship, for crying out loud, with electronic locks. Anyone can come in here, we've proven that. And theres a million miles of ocean around us. Why not actually throw it overboard like she said she was going to?"

"What if it's for safety or security from the murderer?"

"But in this case, she is the murderer. Who would she need

safety or security from?"

James was stumped. "Oh yeah, that's a good point. And she couldn't have carried it with her on board, right?"

"Well, we're not sure. She could have sneaked it on board, I guess."

"But yeah, then why hold on to it? Her job would have been done with killing Jason."

"Obviously, though, it wasn't because she would have killed Aron as well. That's still a huge risk to take and continue taking now."

"What if someone planted it?"

"That is a very real possibility. Although you have to think, this is a horrible plant job. It's reliant on us breaking into her room and searching it and finding a vase in the corner, which then contains it. That's a lot of reliance. On top of all of that, why frame a person who was definitely at dinner with us? Why her?"

"Then what do you think?"

"I'm not sure. Maybe it was a plant. Maybe Sarah forgot about it. Or maybe," Quentin's voice dropped to a whisper. "Maybe she plans on using it again."

James was shocked. *No way. There's no way she wants to use it again. It can't be that.*

"Anyway, I'm going to keep this gun with me. There's no telling what will happen if I leave it here," Quentin said and picked it up and put it inside his coat's pocket. After seeing James' look of disbelief at his cavalier approach to storing the gun, Quentin remarked, "don't worry James. The safety is on, plus I already took out all the bullets. It's empty."

He then departed the room with James following him.

***

Rita's room was next. *This is probably the most normal room we've been in. No excess mess, but not excessively tidy either. She's certainly using her space, though. There's clothes in every part of the wardrobe. Her computer is on the desk and it's somehow logged in? Who taught her computer security?* James noticed.

Quentin noticed the computer, too. He walked over to the desk to see what was open on it. He found some articles Rita was drafting along with some emails directed to the head of finance at a large firm.

"Rita certainly wasn't kidding when she said she was heavily invested in her work. I can see why Jason would have been interested in talking to her. This is some interesting stuff," Quentin remarked.

"But then why drive her away after?"

"I'm not sure. He certainly was a character. Eccentric is an understatement. There's probably something…"

"What?" James asked.

Quentin started looking at the wardrobe. "Nothing, do you see this panel on the wardrobe? It looks out of place, doesn't it?" He walked over to the panel and started prying it off. James went over and started helping him. Together, they pried off the panel in a few minutes. Behind the panel, they found an object that surprised James.

"Another gun?" James exclaimed.

Quentin took out the gun and began to inspect it in silence. A few minutes later, he finished inspecting it and looked up. "Looks like it."

"Is that it? What do you mean looks like it? Of course it looks like a gun. Have you found anything explaining it? I thought we had found our murder weapon last room? "

"I'm not entirely sure. Two bullets are missing from this one, too. So that would mean four bullets were fired, but only two have been found. And we know for a fact that everyone else is alive. So one of these guns was obviously meant to be a plant. But which one?"

"This gun was pretty hard to find."

"True, but sometimes plants have to be hard to find to make them seem more legitimate. I guess we just don't know. I must think on this. Have patience." Quentin then put the gun in his coat's pocket next to the other gun.

James looked mutinous. "Have patience. World's greatest detective," he muttered under his breath.

"What was that, James?" Quentin inquired.

"Nothing." He looked ashamed, obviously not wanting Quentin to have overheard.

"Go on, what is it?"

"It's just this entire case, nothing seems to be going your way. You seem to be getting agitated. You've never really been in control. You almost thought of dropping the case once. I've never seen any of that happen before. You love going around telling everyone you're the best detective in the world, but the murderer here has been one step ahead of you this entire time. Earlier, we had three confessions, each with an airtight alibi. Then, we found out none of them did it. Then, the crime scene disappeared. The security tapes show nothing. Another person gets killed right in front of us and we don't know who did it. Now, we have two murder weapons, but don't know which one is the actual murder weapon. Everyone has a motive, but no one should have the means. There shouldn't have been a single gun on the ship, but we have two. How? I don't know, but that's normal. This time, you don't even know. How am I supposed to have patience? The cruise is coming to an end. We won't be able to hold everyone forever. They'll be let go and then what? How will you find the murderer then?" James said despairingly.

Quentin's eyes widened. "That's it. I think you're on to something. One step ahead of me, of course. Let's keep going. My theory is almost done."

Did he even listen to the rest of what I said? Oh well, James head drooped and he followed Quentin out of the room.

***

The next room was Hemant's. As James expected, the moment they walked in, they saw dumbbells everywhere. *How is this even possible? There's a gym on the ship. How did he even get all these in? And why? I can't imagine he's trying to be a professional bodybuilder. What's wrong with the other gym? After all, he said he was there during the murder anyway. Also, why am I caring so much about this? We're solving a murder and breaking and entering to do so and I'm worried about this guy's gym routine. Also how is everyone still eating dinner, isn't Quentin afraid of beng caught,* James' thoughts were a whirlwind.

Quentin began searching through Hemant's stuff and found packets of instant noodles. "No way, I never would have guessed Hemant was a ramen guy. I mean isn't he supposed to be rich?" James asked.

"These aren't regular noodles, these are Maggi noodles. They're on another level, and are just as bad for you. I had this Indian client earlier who was a billionaire. But as comfort food, he would still continue to have Maggi. It's almost like you can never grow out of it. Everyone has their own process for making it, too. You can use a pot, a microwave, really anything. There's a thousand recipes out there and everyone stands by their recipe. It's a whole culture," Quentin answered.

"Wow ok, I forgot I was trespassing with the British real life equivalent of Wikipedia," James said sounding disgruntled, but secretly continuing to be impressed with Quentin's general knowledge.

Quentin rifled through his one suitcase as well, not finding anything notable other than Aldrich's business card. "Interesting, very interesting," Quentin said to himself.

"Are you going to share what's interesting with me?" James asked.

"No, I don't think I will. Not yet at least, there's something more important to do anyway. But quick question, do you remember how Aldrich said he was connected to Jason?" Quentin asked.

"Yeah, I think so. Something about being old friends, right?" Jason asked.

"That is correct. I'm inclined to believe he's lying, not only do I think they weren't friends, I think Aldrich never saw Jason for many many years before this cruise," Quentin said with an air of importance.

"Why? Then why would he even be here?" James asked.

"That's the real question. Let's find out. Next stop, Aldrich's room," Quentin stated and exited the room.

***

Upon entering Aldrich's room, James and Quentin found it just like a gentleman's room should be. Everything was in its proper place. Aldrich's laptop was on his table neatly plugged into the wall. There was even a cable tie on the power supply. In a drawer of his desk, he had a multitude of handkerchiefs, one for every occasion. There was a happy one, a sad one, an angry one, a pompous one, and an *oh my, there's another murder* one, all in a variety of colors.

"He can open a handkerchief store here. Why is he even in another business? This is his true calling. Look at the handkerchief diversity, one for every situation and color combination," James remarked.

"Indeed. He is a curious fellow, isn't he?" Quentin replied and began searching through the handkerchief mountain. After finding nothing, he continued on to the rest of the desk and tried powering on the laptop.

"Of course there's a password that I can't crack. Well, at least he takes computer security seriously," Quentin said. He then moved on to the bed and inspected it carefully. Finding nothing, the bathroom was the next stop. Once again, everything was kept perfectly. There was perfume from brands James had never heard of before. Quentin looked at them and remarked, "ah I love these perfumes. True British elegance."

James shook his head and continued watching Quentin search the bathroom. After a few minutes, Quentin came out and opened the wardrobe. Inside, there were suits from most designer brands imaginable. Quentin pointed to the watch collection inside. "Those are authentic Rolexes and Patek Philippes. There's even a few Richard Milles on the top. Wow."

"He has a few Rolexes? Whoa."

"Out of the three brands I listed, you focused on Rolex?"

"Yeah, I mean I haven't heard of the others."

"I forget sometimes. The other brands are significantly more expensive and even more pretentious generally. The line goes if you're rich and want to appear rich, you wear a Rolex. If you're uber rich and want just the uber rich to know that, you wear a Patek Philippe or a Richard Mille because most people don't know either brand exists. I'm not sure if Aldrich really has the money, but generally these watches are family watches and passed down throughout the years. I wonder," Quentin explained. He continued searching through the suits that looked like they haven't been worn recently at all. Quentin then hit his hand on something and looked closer. "Well, what do we have here," he exclaimed. He then brushed the suits aside and began lifting a heavy object out. After placing it down, he went back and continued lifting out other objects. Five objects later, he sat down on the bed, exhausted.

"The missing computers! You found them!" James exclaimed.

"Indeed, it looks like Aldrich stole them and hid them back here. I'm not sure why because they were wiped. I wonder if there's any evidence on them," Quentin replied. He then turned on each of the computers and tried accessing them, but they were all wiped. "Why would Aldrich bring them back here? He must have known they were wiped because after all, he had the most to gain from stealing the data. Remember the algorithm Ron mentioned? With that, Aldrich could have made it big again. He must have had access to the room and he had no alibi. That's motive, means, and opportunity. Aron must have been coming to us to tell us about him. There's motive, means, and opportunity there. Except... the murder weapon. Why isn't it here?"

"Well, if he had access to the room, he could have planted it in Sarah's room and one in Rita's room, just in case. On top of that, he wasn't at dinner, remember? He wouldn't have known Sarah was with us," James answered triumphantly.

"Yes, that is plausible. But then why leave such incriminating evidence here? I wonder...," Quentin trailed off, lost in thought. He then snapped back to attention. "I think I know who did the murder, but first I need to check something. Quick, to the dining room."

After saying that, Quentin ran out of the room. James hurried behind him to the dining room where everyone was still eating. Quentin entered the room with a bang, accidentally running into Aldrich. Everyone immediately stopped eating and started staring at Quentin. Quentin looked up at Jason's room and then an expression of delight spread across his face and then he stared back at his captive audience.

I wonder what he saw there. I don't see anything really, James wondered and then paid attention to Quentin again. Like a showman, Quentin had the entire attention of everyone in the room. No one moved a muscle, waiting to see what Quentin would say. Quentin soaked it in, took a deep breath, and then announced, "I know who the murderer is!"

10

Everyone stared at Quentin. Then, after a few seconds, everyone burst out yelling, clamoring to get Quentin's attention.

"What do you mean you know who the murderer is?" Ash yelled.

"Wait, does this mean we can finally try to enjoy the cruise?" Samantha asked.

"Is the murderer somewhere in the room?" Danny asked, glancing around him nervously.

"Everyone, calm down. Quentin will say it sooner or later," Ron said lazily.

"I'm not going to calm down. At least finally people will stop accusing me," Ash retorted.

"I'm just terrified of the murderer being one of us. Who knows how they'll react?" Rita mentioned.

"Golly, at long last, one of you professional detectives have accomplished the relatively simplistic task of identified the individual responsible for Jason's untimely death," Aldrich commented.

"So are you going to tell us who did it? Who killed Jason and Aron?" Sarah asked. Everyone stopped talking and started looking expectantly at Quentin.

"I don't know who the murderer is," Quentin announced with the same confidence.

"Say what?" Hemant asked incredulously.

"You just said you did. What do you mean you don't know who the murderer is?" Ash yelled again.

"Does this mean we have to go back to living in fear one this cruise?" Samantha asked.

"Everyone, stop talking. Let Quentin at least talk. He'll explain everything," James ordered. *At least I think he will. He certainly likes the attention.*

"Thank you James. I was going to say I don't know who the murderer is, but I will know in a little bit. You see, Jason's computers have webcams. They recorded the entire murder and of course everything after, including when they were stolen. Of course, the murderer was smart. They wiped the computers. Except, on further investigation, one of the computers wasn't wiped. I was going to go back to the computers to watch the recording, but then the computers were stolen. However, I have an idea who stole the computers. And the computers are in their room, currently. Isn't that right, Aldrich?" Quentin said, turning to Aldrich. *What is he playing at? The computers were all wiped or we would have checked them out?* James wondered.

"Me? I did no such thing. I did not lay a hand on any computational devices whatsoever. Identify some different individual to become a scapegoat, I shall not be the scapegoat to your diabolical witch-hunt," Aldrich said indignantly.

"Okay, this is an easy one to prove. Give me your room key and I'll check your room for those computers," Quentin replied.

Aldrich began searching his pockets and then looked back at Quentin with a look of surprise on his face. "I would but I do not have my key with me at present. I must have misplaced it. Either way, what I have in my room is confidential. You should not be privy to such information anyway."

"Of course, you lost your key. What a time to lose it, too. No matter, I can go to the captain's office to get their master key. In the meantime, I implore you all to go to your rooms and stay there until I call for you. We don't know what the murderer will do now that they are almost going to be exposed. Aldrich, since you conveniently don't have your key, you can just hang around here," Quentin said scathingly.

Everyone began to get up and move out of the dining room in silence. After thirty seconds, everyone had left to go to their respective rooms. "Come James, let's go get the master key," Quentin said and walked out of the dining room. James followed him. After they had walked a few steps, Quentin doubled back and took a turn to go down the hallway towards the staterooms and away from the captain's office.

"Quentin, what are you doing? We know the computers don't have anything. And you have the master key. What was the point of all that?" James asked.

"I'm glad you didn't say anything. I'm trying to catch the killer redhanded. It's the oldest story in the book. Make up some evidence that's essential to finding the murderer. They'll go back to wipe the footage and we'll catch them in the act," Quentin replied.

"But that's so obvious. What if they don't go back?"

"They will. Even if they think it's a trick, as you said, they think they're smarter than us. They think they're one step ahead of me. This is something unexpected for them. They thought they had wiped all the computers but a small part of them will always wonder if they missed something. And if that something will be their downfall. It's so difficult for them to sit there and be okay with taking that risk. They need to be in control of everything and that includes removing all evidence. So they will definitely go back and we will catch them."

James was still skeptical. *If this murderer is so smart, will he really fall for this? Then again, Quentin should have more experience in this, so I guess he knows best. What if the murderer runs or tries to fight? Should I be prepared to take out my orange-belt taekwondo lessons?*

Quentin and James crept slowly towards Aldrich's room. There was pure silence throughout the hallway. James felt as if the hallway had elongated. His heart was racing. Every door seemed to make a creak. Every step seemed to produce a different sound. He didn't know what they would find when they got to Aldrich's room, but he wanted to be prepared for everything. More than likely, it would be nothing, but if there was someone, it would be a cold-blooded murderer who had already murdered two people. After what felt like an eternity, Quentin raised his hand to stop James. He pointed at the door. *Aldrich's door*, James realized. James listened closely and heard some typing noises inside. Quentin looked excited and pulled out his master key and unlocked the door and slowly opened it.

Inside, the computers were pulled out and a hooded figure was sitting, typing furiously on each of the computer to try and log in. James' heart was stuck in his throat. He couldn't speak or move. *This is it. This is the person who killed two people. Maybe I should have gotten past an orange belt after all.* The figure had not heard them enter and was still focused solely on the computers. Their typing was getting faster and angrier, almost as if they were just understanding that they were tricked. The figure finished typing on all the computers and looked from left to right to see if there was any other computer they had missed. After finding no such extra computer, they let out a groan of frustration and then began to turn around to leave.

"Going somewhere?" Quentin challenged with an air of

authority. *He's having fun with this, isn't he? I'm here terrified and he looks like Christmas came early.*

The figure turned and saw them for the first time. For a while, Quentin and James just looked at the figure. The figure looked back. Both parties kept waiting for the other one to make the first move. Neither wanted to move first. The figure looked cornered, but James thought that made them look even more dangerous. The tension grew more palpable. Eventually, the figure began to make slight movements, almost as if testing the waters without breaking anything. And then, all of a sudden, the figure jumped up and sprinted towards Quentin and James. Quentin went out to stop him, but the figure ducked beneath Quentin's outstretched arm and in no time, was already behind them and outside of the room and continued sprinting out the hallway.

Quentin looked surprised, turned around, and then ran after the figure. James stopped to appreciate the figure. *Wow, they must have been a legend at tag when they were kids. Look at that duck, that dodge, that swerve.*

"Hey James, care to join me?" Quentin called while running.

"Oh yeah, coming," James responded and began to follow Quentin.

The three of them kept running through hallway after hallway. The figure never relented and Quentin certainly wasn't going to give up. James kept trying to keep up, grumbling under his breath. *I wish we had just closed the door then. But no, Quentin had to be the hero. Now I have to run a marathon at Usain Bolt's speed. Who even is this person? What did they eat for dinner that they can run like this now?*

After a few more hallways, James began to notice that they were in a part of the ship where he had never set foot in yet. *This is the engine room!*

"James, careful. I lost them," Quentin called with a note of fear in his voice. *Where can they be?* James wondered. The two of them slowly branched out, keeping each other in their sights at all times, scouring the room for the figure. *Wait, why am I looking for them again? I'm just a guy. They'll probably beat me up and continue running, it's not like I can do anything. Why and how did I get caught in this?* James cursed himself.

There was a sound of a can being kicked in the far corner of the room. Both Quentin and James turned towards the sound. James saw a flash out of the corner of his eye. *The person tricked us, he's behind Quentin.* James opened his mouth to warn Quentin when the figure kicked Quentin and ran out the door that they came in. James ran over to Quentin to help him up.

"Are you okay?" James asked.

"No, I most certainly am not okay. He tricked me, kicked me, and flicked me. It's all the icks! Let's go after him, come on!" Quentin exclaimed angrily.

As they ran towards the door, they saw the figure close the door behind them. James ran to the door to try to open it. It was locked. "Oh no, he's locked us in here! We're going to die alone here, aren't we?" James said in despair.

"Relax, we have the key, remember?" Quentin mentioned and then calmly took out the key and unlocked the door. "Come on, I didn't think you would be one to panic so easily. Now which way would he have gone?"

James saw a flash of black at the end of the hallway and pointed at it. "Let's go!" Quentin said and began sprinting after him with James in tow.

They sprinted behind the person towards the dining room. *Come on, how are Quentin and the person not tired yet?* James thought.

Eventually, the dining room got closer and closer. Near the entry of the dining room, out of nowhere, Aldrich appeared and tripped the figure as they were running into the room.

The figure fell down and James had barely had time to appreciate the stop when with all the commotion, everyone came out of their rooms and started streaming into the dining room. The hood had fallen back to reveal the identity of the figure who had run laps around the ship. Everyone gasped, including James. Except for Quentin, that is. He looked absolutely delighted with a knowing look on his face. *There's no way he knew this. Right?* James wondered.

Eventually, the figure got up and pulled the hood back, defeated. It was a man who looked confident despite knowing he had just lost. He straightened up and looked at the rest of the crowd, not saying a word.

"Danny!" Sarah shrieked.

Quentin took a moment to survey the crowd and waited for the whispering to die down before talking. "Yes, Danny. Or really, should I say, Jason Spark?"

11

Everyone stood shocked for a few seconds. *What? Jason Spark? How is that possible?* James thought, bewildered.

"What do you mean Jason Spark?" Ash called out.

"Didn't he die? Wasn't that the whole thing?" Rita continued.

"No way, are you actually Jason Spark?" Ron asked to Danny. *No, not Danny, Jason.*

Danny surveyed the crowd, calm for once. When he began to speak, his voice rung out over the crowd with the air of someone who was used to commanding attention. "Quentin is indeed correct. I am Jason Spark."

Everyone was stunned silent once again. Quentin took the opportunity to begin to move inside the dining room, corralling everyone inside. Everyone sat down at a table except for Jason, Quentin, and James, who were standing and looking at the crowd.

"So if this is Jason, who was the person who died earlier?" Hemant asked.

"Good question Hemant. Would Jason care to give that answer?" Quentin responded.

Jason looked at Quentin with a combination of disgust and interest. "No, I don't think I shall. I want to hear what you have gathered, oh world's greatest detective."

Quentin's eyes narrowed and he looked slightly disgruntled, but his eyes betrayed delight. *He knew Jason would respond like that. Quentin just loves the attention and he's not regretting explaining everything at all*, James realized.

Quentin cleared his throat and looked around the room to make sure everyone was paying attention to him. "Let me paint a story for you guys. There was once a man who was super intelligent. He created various algorithms to make billions. He now wanted to go public to make even more money at any cost. But there were two issues. First, he had a godfather in the industry who had sheltered him, but was also a direct competitor. Second, his business partner. Someone who knew too much information about apparently a secret algorithm designed to outcompete all competitors."

This is Ron's story about Jason and Danny. No way, how is this relevant?

Ron looked very interested all of a sudden in this story while everyone else were bewildered at this story.

"Quentin, I love the story, but what does this have to do with Jason and the murder?" Samantha asked.

"Don't worry, I'm getting there," Quentin responded and then continued. "Now, how else to make the business big to make even more money? He had to remove both people from the equation without suspicion. The business partner was easy. He owned none of the stock, so just had to incriminate him in some crime and he would be gone forever. Or mostly forever. The godfather was slightly harder. He was old, yes, but he had influence and money. He couldn't simply be incriminated falsely, he needed to be out of the picture, permanently. This man had to do what he could to ensure his wallet's security after all, so he did the unthinkable. He ensured the godfather could not get in his way ever again."

With this, Aldrich immediately turned pale and began

gasping for air. Quentin turned to Aldrich. "Yes, Aldrich. Your father was erased by Jason."

"Is this actually true Jason?" Aldrich asked when he was able to form words again, all pompousness gone.

"I'm afraid it is. I needed him out of the way. My business wasn't being taken seriously by anyone because of him," Jason responded.

"But we were family friends. I have not seen you in decades, but we grew up together. My father supported you when you were alone. He took you in, gave you a home, gave you a family, and this is how you repaid him?" Aldrich asked despairingly, his words choking in his throat. *Who would have thought Aldrich actually had emotions? Whoa,* James thought.

"This type of sentimentality is what kept you from becoming a good businessman. Don't you remember when we were children how I would always say I would become a big businessman and you would always say you wanted to become like your father? That was when I decided I needed to be bigger than he ever was and if he must go for that, then he must go," Jason replied coldly.

Quentin waited for them to finish and then continued the story. "Many of you remember my story in the beginning of the cruise. That murder was of the founder of Appleton Technologies, Aldrich's father. Jason was in the hotel then and he was the one who brutally murdered Mr. Appleton."

"Don't you guys remember how Jason kept interrupting Quentin when he was telling his story?" Ash pointed out. "I knew he was bad news then."

"You really want to take credit for this, don't you?" Ron commented.

"Hey, you were the one socializing constantly with Jason, a murderer," Sarah said scathingly.

"Quentin, how did you realize it was Jason who killed Mr. Appleton?" Rita asked, raising her voice to be heard over everyone else.

"Well Rita, it was a combination of things. First, I had known the history between the Appletons and Jason. It was why when I saw Aldrich, I knew something was up. The coincidence is too unlikely. Second, Ron told me this interesting story about how Jason had a godfather who helped him through his business and the industry. Then, Aldrich walked in saying he knew Jason from a long time ago, implying they were family friends. Third, and most critically, during my investigation, I found many copies of the exact same calling card used in the hotel murder in Jason's room. This along with the pseudonym, Ember vs Spark, confirmed it to me that Jason was the one who killed Mr. Appleton," Quentin explained.

"This still doesn't answer the question about the actual murders," Ron mentioned.

"Hey, give him a chance. It doesn't help if you keep cutting in," Samantha retorted.

"Thank you, Samantha. Don't worry Ron, trust me. This story is extremely vital for the events of this week. It was the plan that had set everything in motion. Only two people on this cruise were here as direct invitations by Jason, Aldrich and myself," Quentin stated.

"You're forgetting about Rita and me," Sarah pointed out.

"Sorry, good point. I meant two people who were given a mysterious invitation. The two of you were given a reason. Aldrich was invited by the last person he would have expected. I was invited to solve a crime, but was given no extra details. This got me thinking, why would a murderer who knew I had almost caught him invite me personally?"

"Almost catching me is a stretch. You weren't close at all. I was way ahead of you the entire time in the hotel," Danny stated.

Quentin ignored the interruption. "Anyway, when I got

here, I realized Aldrich was given an invitation, too, and that got me thinking, why would he invite his worst enemy, the son of the man Jason betrayed and killed? Especially because Aldrich was in charge of the business in direct competition with Jason's. Nothing was adding up. This wasn't helped by the murder, either. But then I realized, what if the crime wasn't the murder, but something else? Then, Ron's story about the rumors of a vastly superior algorithm that only Jason had on his home computer came up. That computer which must be on the ship. Soon, the dastardly plan was slowly getting pieced together. Jason baited Aldrich to come onto the ship, knowing Aldrich could never reject a chance to get the algorithm. Jason knew Aldrich would attempt to steal the algorithm and in the process would be caught by yours truly. Then, for corporate espionage, theft, breaking and entering, etc, Aldrich would be imprisoned, causing the dissolution of his business. Even if he were to get out on bail, no investor would trust his company anymore and it would be finished. To Jason's credit, Aldrich took the bait and came on board with the sole intention of stealing the files. In fact, he was the one who wiped the computers in the first place, isn't that right?"

Aldrich turned pale and began sweating. He took out his handkerchief for use in guilty situations and began wiping his face. Then he hung his head and explained. "Yes, you are correct. I came here to steal the files and when I realized he was out of his room, I went on his computer and tried finding the algorithm. I could not find it, so to be sure, I just erased all the files on all of his computers and left. But I swear, I did nothing else."

Quentin nodded. "Don't worry, I know. This is where Aron came in use. He was someone who was broke and who needed the money. Aldrich utilized him to steal the files. Aron was coming to tell us that when he was shot."

"So you're saying Aldrich shot Aron? But I thought Jason was the murderer," Hemant said confused.

"What about the first body though? Who's that?" Samantha asked.

"Don't worry, I'll explain both of your questions soon enough. First, let's unravel this mystery. You see, a lot of things should be lining up, but weren't. Aldrich stole the files, Aron helped him, Aldrich logically would have shot Aron to cover up loose ends. But then, what were the computers doing in Aldrich's room if he didn't find any files on them anyway? He knew they were wiped. Why risk it? The security footage posed other questions. We found Aron's card to be used to access Jason's room to steal those files. But Aldrich's card was never added, so if he didn't have master key access, how could he have shot Aron because we found the murder weapon in either Sarah's room or Rita's room? Each fact shot up more questions. So to unravel everything, we must first start with one mystery, the root event. Then, that will lead us to the other mysteries, or will at least keep posing questions that will eventually solve the whole story," Quentin explained.

"Wait, what do you mean the murder weapon was found in my room?" Rita asked.

"And my room?" Sarah continued.

"Did you go through our rooms without permission?" Rita asked indignantly.

"Ah yes. I forgot I haven't mentioned that part. I did. The captain gave me access. Don't worry, I haven't stolen anything, but it was necessary to find the culprit. Without it, I would never have known the computers were in Aldrich's room and I never would have caught Jason. So I do apologize for intruding on your privacy, but it was needed. And yes, I found two guns. Both were missing two bullets. One was found in Sarah's room and one was found in Rita's room.

Don't worry, I'll get to that later," Quentin responded slightly ashamed.

Sarah looked understanding and began nodding. Rita still looked mutinous, but motioned for Quentin to carry on. Quentin took a look at them apologetically and then continued. "So let's continue with this mystery. Aldrich knew how to hack computers, we know this. So he added Aron's credentials to access Jason's room. This way, even if the hack was identified, it wouldn't be traced back to him. Then, he looped the security footage, so we wouldn't find out that Aron visited Jason's room around 12-2 PM the day the first murder occurred. These are known at this point. So now, the next question, what are the computers doing there?"

Quentin looked expectantly at the crowd, attempting to make this interactive. Ash raised his hand. "Yes, Ash?" Quentin asked.

"Is it to draw more attention to Aldrich as a frame job?" Ash ventured.

"Indeed. This was done by Jason. Remember, his main goal was to get Aldrich out of the way and he has already proven that nothing stops him from achieving his goals one way or another. He took the computers out of the crime scene and moved them to Aldrich's room to frame him even more. Since this was his cruise, he still had his master key with him to access Aldrich's room. However, even with that, we weren't searching rooms yet so we hadn't seen the computers. Jason's now getting desperate, he needs Aldrich out of the way and he needs the blame to go on Aldrich then. The entire ship knew Aldrich and Aron had been getting into arguments and Jason knew iii was because of Aron getting cold feet with the plan. What better way to remove Aldrich than frame him in a murder? So Jason killed Aron in front of us. This served two purposes. It could discourage me and forced me to not realize that Jason's still alive, especially because at this point, he knew I had seen the cards and knew he had killed Mr. Appleton. Or it could embolden me to find a culprit as soon as possible and the best culprit available was Aldrich. Two birds one stone. Isn't that right Jason?" Quentin began to look at Jason expectantly.

"Again, that is right. I killed Aron. Again, nobody stands in my way. First Aldrich's father. Then Aldrich. He needed to go. On top of that, Aron had the audacity of breaking into my room and stealing my files? He deserved to die," Jason said apathetically.

Samantha was shaking with rage. "He was my friend, we've been through so much together, all the competitions, everything. And you say he deserved to die? For a thing you set up? What even is this algorithm?"

"Samantha, as a matter of fact, there is no algorithm. Right, Jason?" Quentin said.

"Once again, correct. I'm surprised so many people thought such an algorithm exists. You all love to think that computer science can create magic. Well, newsflash, it doesn't. There's not a magic silver algorithm that lets you outcompete everyone. You have to be more ruthless than anyone else in the industry. I outcompeted everyone the old fashioned way, lobbying more than every other company. I just spread that rumor around to confuse everyone and you all bought it. That is, except for you Quentin. It took you a matter of minutes to find out what all these idiots couldn't for years," Jason replied.

"Oh yeah, lobbying. Modern and legal corruption. Makes perfect sense," Ash realized.

"So that explains Aron's death. What about the gun though?" Hemant asked.

"You're on fire with your questions today, Hemant," Quentin replied. "Jason brought on board a few guns with him just in case. Since it was his ship, he got through security without a hitch. After Aron's death, he knew he had to throw suspicion off. He knew that Rita would be a perfect suspect because everyone had heard her arguing with the first victim and she wasn't at dinner with us, so he planted the gun in her room after killing Aron."

"So back then to who was the first victim, the supposed Jason?" Rita asked.

"This was the final part of Jason's plan. He needed to be on the outside, so he could ensure his plan works perfectly. He didn't want to be the center of attention, as he knew Aldrich would wait for him to leave the room before stealing anything. From the outside, he could watch in the shadows as his plan worked. To do that, he needed someone else to be Jason for the cruise. Now, who could that be? It had to be someone who knew what he looked like and someone who needed money desperately to agree to this. It also had to be someone who wouldn't be treated seriously by any authorities in case they tried to betray Jason. Only one person fits the bill, to serve as Jason's puppet, the real Danny," Quentin answered.

"So it was Danny who died in the beginning?" Ron asked.

"That is correct," Quentin nodded.

"How did you know this switch happened?" Ash asked.

"Remember Jason's most defining trait? He freaked out when someone asked to take his picture. For a while, I thought that was just because he was reclusive, but then Ron mentioned something about how no one actually knew who he was and he was almost like a legend, a myth. Then, it hit me, why were we assuming this was Jason Spark just off of him giving a speech in the beginning of the cruise? No one had seen him before. I'm assuming that meant the cruise staff as well or they were in on it. Either way, if he wasn't Jason, then where was Jason? And then another thing Ron said struck me, that Jason ruined Danny's life as well. Why would

Danny have come to Jason's cruise then?

"Then, there were the differences between Jason prior to the cruise and the Jason everyone had met on the cruise. Before the cruise, he invited Sarah and Rita to celebrate their accomplishments in chemistry and economics, respectively. But all of a sudden, he began to attack them on the ship, saying they couldn't truly be experts in either field? The personality switch made me more inclined to believe as time went on that Jason wasn't really Jason. And if Jason wasn't really Jason, then Danny would have been the only one to identify that and he didn't say a word, so there must have been a switch somewhere.

"Finally, the security card. Only Jason had the master key. It didn't make sense that someone seemed to almost pass through all the walls of each room like a ghost without the master key. What better way to become a ghost than to not be yourself, but still possess all the access your position gives you?" Quentin explained.

No way, this plan was so complicated. How did Jason almost pull it off? It sounds like there were so many places where it could have been destroyed. Either he's very good or just very lucky, James thought. "Why didn't you just steal financial data from Aldrich and report him to the IRS? An import-export business doesn't sound very legal for tax reasons," he commented.

Jason was so stunned he couldn't speak. When he gathered his wits, he replied. "I guess I never thought about that. I thought my plan would work."

"Hey, whose business are you calling illegal?" Aldrich challenged and stood up.

"Yours, you were the one who did try to steal data from Jason and failed because it didn't exist. Sit down, you're not sounding very smart right now. You too Jason. Your plan hinged on Aldrich taking your bait, then successfully stealing something, and then Quentin being there to catch it. I mean, there were so many parts where you could have failed because you're not in control of this at all. You're completely reliant on other people. You even got a whole body double for this one thing. Way to overcomplicate stuff. Then, when your plan wasn't working, you killed someone just to get Quentin's attention. How desperate are you? Honestly, if the two of you are some of the smartest and richest people on the planet, we got issues," James ranted.

Quentin was trying hard to hide his laughter at this outburst. When he finally got in control of his emotions, he straightened up and replied. "I knew you had it in you, James. Now you see why you're so useful? They should be consulting you next time."

"Random question, though. Jason was with us during dinner when Danny was killed. How and why did he kill Danny?" Ron pointed out.

"Oh yeah, that is a good question. I remember him, too," Samantha commented.

"There's no way he could have teleported there and back, it's impossible," Ash mentioned.

"But he did trick us with everything else, he also knew the ship inside and out, maybe he did some trickery," Ron said.

"You know, I'm forgetting if he was actually there," Sarah said.

"Oh no, he was. I was talking to him, remember?" Ron replied.

"Are you sure he was there the entire time?" Sarah shot back.

"I guess, I don't really remember the time. It was a while ago—" Ron said.

"Stop! Regardless of how ruthless I am, I did not kill Danny. Did I care he was dead? No. Did I do it? No," Jason interrupted.

"Why should we even believe you? You were playing us

the entire cruise," Ash said.

"Yeah, I'm not sure you're the most reputable of sources right now," Rita said.

"We won't listen to anything you say anyway," Hemant added.

Jason stopped talking and just stared angrily at the crowd. As everyone kept discussing how he could have done it, Quentin raised his hand for silence. Everyone stopped talking and looked at him as he began to speak again. "In this case, you are correct Ron. He was there, I distinctly remember. In fact, a large portion of the cruise was there, too. It couldn't have been him. Jason's telling the truth this time. Well, mostly. I do believe he cared that Danny was dead. Did he care because Danny was a person? Of course not. He cared solely because Danny's murder put a wrench in his plans.

"We spent the entire investigation thinking that Danny's murder and Aron's murder were connected and that Aron was killed to hide Danny's murderer. Why was that an automatic assumption? I must confess, I don't know. I made the same assumption you all did. I thought the two murders had to be connected causally, but then I realized what if they were connected, not by the perpetrator, but by something else? When Danny was killed, it happened at the same time as when Aldrich had stolen the files. I believe that was a coincidence. The true perpetrator had no idea that Aldrich was stealing the files at all, let alone that day. Jason was delighted that the beginning of his plan was working. Jason would plant the computers in Aldrich's room. Now all he needed was Danny to mention to me the next day that the computers are missing. I would naturally find them in Aldrich's room and the plan completed to fruition.

"But when Danny died, the computers were still there. Jason hadn't had time to move them, yet. Now, we think it has to do with the murder, but it doesn't make sense for the computers to be in Aldrich's room. After all, they were wiped. All our focus was now on the murder, not the potential espionage, and more importantly, we attributed the espionage as a motive for the murder, not as two separate events. Jason didn't plan this. That's why he had to kill Aron. He would have been the last person to kill Danny, at least at that time. He needed Danny for his plan.

"Once I realized that Jason had nothing to do with Danny's death, I revisited some more assumptions. First, the assumption in the beginning before we knew about the switch that Jason was the target. What if Jason wasn't the target, but Danny was? And if so, why? Second, who's to say that just because we heard the body drop at 7 that that was when he was killed? After all, we immediately went to the room and it was empty. That was the whole crux of the locked room mystery."

"But Quentin, you had seen a shadow remember? That's why you went up?" James asked.

"That's correct. I did. From the ground, it looked like somebody was in the room. However, I know for a fact that the room is empty now, but look up at the window," Quentin ordered.

Everyone turned to look at the window. There was a shadow fluttering just like that day as if someone was there. "But how?" Rita asked.

"Do you see the chandelier in the middle? The light from around the chandelier isn't symmetric for some reason and is constantly pulsing. The shadow is from that and it's moving due to the asymmetry and pulsing nature of the light. The shadow isn't significant at all," Quentin answered.

"So then it could be anyone?" Hemant asked.

"Sort of. At that point, I had ruled out Aldrich and Aron and Jason, of course. I started focusing on the first assumption. What if Danny was the target? Who could have a vendetta against him?" Quentin replied and began walking in the center of the room. James turned to him with everyone behind him also keeping their eyes solely on Quentin.

"And then I remembered a story. A story of love. A story of grief. A story of betrayal and deceit. And then I knew who killed Danny," Quentin started.

"No—you couldn't have known. It wasn't supposed to be like this. How did you know?" A voice from behind James cried out in anguish.

12

James whirled around to see Sarah trembling. She was the one who had spoken out. Everyone was looking at her in shock. *Sarah? But she was so sweet this entire time,* James thought.

"I'm sorry Sarah. I couldn't let it go. As much as I wish I could," Quentin said gently.

"How did you know?" Sarah asked barely holding it together.

"Sarah? You did this?" Samantha asked in disbelief.

"Samantha, give her some time," Quentin cut in. "Let me recount the story for those who don't know. Sarah had met this guy she fell in love with some years ago. He was going to marry her, but on the way to the altar, drowned in a fishing accident. Sarah was heartbroken and almost committed suicide. She eventually got control over her life again after many years and became a very successful chemist and was invited on this cruise. Imagine her shock when she found her true love alive and well posing as Jason Spark."

"Wait, you mean Danny was that guy from back then? He left her and didn't have the guts to tell her to her face?" Rita asked.

"Correct. Danny was being investigated by the FBI for

money laundering for a while at that point and he knew that if Sarah found out he was a criminal, she would ostracize him. In his mind, for some reason, he cared more about having a better reputation with Sarah even if she thought he was dead, so he disappeared, leaving her to bear the brunt of his actions," Quentin said.

"I loved him! When I saw him on the cruise, I couldn't bear it. How could he leave me?" Sarah responded in anguish, tears streaming. "He didn't even know what...what state he left me in. My life was almost over because of him. If he wanted to leave me, then fine, but I grieved for him. I mourned him. I was in grief for years and still was until now. I would occasionally think of him and think about how my life would be different if he was still alive and with me. I would remember the tiny things like when he got me gifts or surprised me. I would remember phrases he would say. I would watch his favorite movie every year and remember how he reacted to the movie when he showed it to me. I would remember his little quirks. I would remember all of that and realize he would never be there, not anymore. Until I saw him that day. But how did you know Quentin that it was me?"

"Once I realized that Danny could have been the intended target, I thought about who could possibly have a motive to kill Danny and does it have something to do with the story you told James. Then I started thinking about the main problem of this crime. How was the door bolted, but no one inside? And how did the killer disappear? I realized the second part had to do with the time that Jason had died earlier, probably at 6:30 PM when housekeeping showed up at his door. After all, there was no housekeeping sent that day, so someone had to have posed at housekeeping and killed him. So if Jason had been shot at 6:30, it's significantly more likely that the perpetrator was at dinner with us because it's the perfect alibi," Quentin explained. "So that left me with a few main suspects: Ron, Ash, Samantha, and you, Sarah. Ash had picked up an SD card at the crime scene, which I quickly realized actually belonged to Aron when he had broken in earlier in the day. In order to cause Danny's body to drop at 7:00, it meant the killer was skilled with putting together some contraption for that purpose.

"I had no idea what that was yet, but I couldn't imagine why Ash would have wanted to kill Danny and his expertise was in psychiatry, not really the most hands-on science. Ron was purely in computer science, so I would have imagined if he even wanted to break in, he would have hacked the security feeds just like Aldrich did. On top of that, he is too tall to be the housekeeper. That left Samantha and Sarah. This was where I was stuck, so I endeavored to solve the mystery of the locked door and how Danny's body dropped at 7 instead of 6:30."

"The room was trashed too, remember?" James asked.

"That too. You see they were all connected. Sarah wanted to make the crime scene as dirty as possible. She first entered the room and picked up one of Jason's guns that was still in the room and shot Danny. Then, she trashed the room to obscure any evidence she might have left. She then placed Danny on the chair and positioned him near the balcony so with a strong enough hit, he would fall down. Now, she needed to make sure the door was locked and bolted from the inside to further confirm her alibi as just having dinner. She first thought of using a magnet, but soon realized that the bolt is made of gold and thus isn't magnetic. She then remembered Danny's fondness for fishing. They were on a ship after all; he had to have fishing line somewhere. She went hunting and found some fishing line.

"She knew the chemical properties of the fishing line and the material it was made of so she knew exactly how strong it was and how long it would take to burn. Especially because she knew Danny used braided fishing lines, which are made of fabric and actually burn and don't melt unlike conventional fishing lines, which are made of plastic. She saw the fireworks in the corner, which were meant to be used at the end of the cruise, and took one firecracker out and positioned it directly in front of the chair. She attached one fishing line from one end of the firecracker to the bolt. Because of the angle and the strength of braided fishing lines, which are rated sometimes at almost 500 pounds, when the firecracker is set off, the bolt gets slammed shut. It does damage the bolt slightly, but when we were going to break down the door anyway, it would still give the same impression of a completely bolted door.

"She then attached another section of fishing line to the firecracker, lighting it on fire exactly so it will burn out in thirty minutes, causing the firecracker to go off, producing that large noise at 7 PM. The firecracker went off and hit Danny and caused him to fall down. The moment I saw the firecracker, I realized that that was used to push Danny off the balcony because a bullet is too small to do so. Now only one person on the cruise knows this much about chemistry and physics to create some device like that, and that was Sarah," Quentin stated.

"But then why would she keep the gun in her room and also confess?" James asked bewildered.

"Great question. This was the extra cunning part of Sarah's plan. By confessing in the beginning, she wanted to draw attention to herself. She then lied about the gunshot wound, knife wound, and what she did with the murder weapon to make it seem like she was innocent, but covering for someone. She knew we knew she had an alibi. This way, we would never suspect her again. To further that, she kept the gun in her room the entire time. She didn't have a way of accessing other rooms to plant it, and again, because her alibi was air-tight, she knew we would assume someone planted it. In this case, one of the obvious suspects actually did do it, and she leaned into the obviousness to hide her crime. Of course, Jason's plan further enabled her, but that was pure luck," Quentin finished.

"I'm sorry guys, I really am. I didn't want to do it, but seeing him just made me remember all of those countless dark days and nights and I couldn't let him get away with it. Do I regret it? No, he deserved it. But I am sorry I ruined all of your guys vacations. I didn't mean for it to get this out of hand," Sarah said wiping tears from her eyes.

"It's okay, Sarah. I understand and I'm sure the rest of us do, too," Ash mentioned.

Sarah's eyes lit up and she wordlessly walked back to her room as the rest of the room looked uneasily at each other, happy they had found the murderer at last, but upset about how it played out.

13

The next day was the final day of the cruise. James was still reeling from the previous day's events. *I can't believe there was so much drama going on. Two murderers that managed to somehow get in each other's way and make the case more complicated by the end! Maybe Quentin was right about being the world's greatest detective, I'm not sure the case would have been solved without him. I do feel awful for Sarah, however. I could feel the raw emotion and anguish when she was talking to me about the story a few days ago and her reaction last night. I hope a jury is nice to her. Although, finally, Jason is going to jail even with his connections and money. He finally got what he deserved after so long.*

James got out of his room, completely packed, and walked to the dining hall where everyone was clustering to say goodbye to each other. *We won't forget this trip for a long time. After all, the best connections are forged in a ship full of crime and murder.*

He saw Ash and Samantha talking at a table. At the next table, Rita and Hemant were eating together. James overheard them talking about some finance related terms that he didn't fully understand. Ron and Aldrich were talking fervently at a third table. James saw Ron pass Aldrich a business card and a resume. *He's still trying for a new job, isn't he? Well, hopefully he gets it.*

At the final table, Quentin was sitting alone, observing the hall. James went and sat down next to him. "So Quentin, how are you feeling now that you solved the case?" He asked.

"Honestly, James, it's bittersweet. It's definitely satisfying to finally catch Jason, but if I had caught him at the hotel or even earlier in the trip, Aron would still be alive today and be eating with us. It's a hard line. It's always satisfying to catch murderers, but then I always realize that I'm only solving murders, I'm not preventing them. People are being killed every time and I'm getting them justice after the fact. It's not helping them stay alive. So every time I finish a case, I appreciate having solved it, but also regret that someone had to die in order for me to feel that way," Quentin responded despondently.

"You said it yourself, if you had caught Jason at the hotel, Aron would still be here today," James said.

"That's supposed to make me feel better? If so, you really need to go get some more books on optimism and motivation."

"Just remember, every time you catch a murderer like Jason now, you're preventing other future murders. Now Jason can't go and kill someone else just to further his company and greed. Only because of you," James continued.

"I know and that is the classic explanation everyone gives. But what about Sarah? She was a good person. But she still killed someone. Danny wasn't a good person, either, but he didn't deserve to die. But Sarah also doesn't deserve to have her life ruined because of that, right? She wouldn't have killed anyone else after this. Solving that murder didn't help anyone. Danny's still dead and I didn't stop any future murder, so what's really the point? It's not our job to judge whether someone is right or not, but I can't help but wonder if I'm really helping," Quentin continued sadly.

James was lost for words. *Is Quentin right? All those cop shows I used to watch, all those mysteries I used to read. Are they sometimes really not helping? I'm not even sure, how are we supposed to know beforehand if someone is a "good" person or someone like Jason who would continue until someone stopped him? This is obviously something Quentin thought about multiple times, but he still continues. Maybe he is right, that its just always going to be bittersweet and that's just the reality of solving these cases and we just try what we can.*

James opened his mouth to reply, but then saw Quentin just looking lost in thought. *Nothing I say will go into his ears now. I might as well go and talk to everyone else before we dock.* He walked over to Ron and Aldrich's table.

"So what are you guys going to do now?" James asked.

"Well, Spark Industries needs a new CEO imminently. I will be in contact with the board to ascertain if I could be of any service or if there is a potential acquisition in the works now. It will be a great deal of work; however, I have hope that with this move, I can achieve my late father's dream of his company being the most successful technological firm in the world," Aldrich replied.

"I'm hoping to get a job at Aldrich's company now. I can finally get away from my current job. I absolutely hate it," Ron replied vehemently.

"What about you and Quentin?" Aldrich asked.

"I'm not sure. Every previous mystery, we just kind of go to our homes and then just hang out until we get another call. However, somehow, wherever we go, even on vacation, there's always mystery around, so I have complete faith that we will have another case in the future," James answered.

"Well, good luck to you. Thanks to you two, we ended up catching two murderers. Hopefully, you can continue that in the future as well," Ron said.

"Why is Quentin sitting like that in the corner?" Rita asked while walking up to their table with Hemant in tow.

"He's just kinda sad about how it all worked out, so I left him alone with his thoughts," James replied. "What about you two? What are your plans now that the cruise is over?"

"Well, I for one am getting another ticket. This was supposed to be a vacation, not a place to be stressed out for days. Plus I was supposed to get Jason as a client, but that's obviously useless now. And then after that, I'll continue with my life, I guess. I feel bad for Sarah, though," Hemant answered.

"Yeah, me too. She seemed so nice and definitely not the murderous type. I really wish she didn't have to go to jail. I think I'll miss her," Rita commented.

"Yeah that's exactly why Quentin's so sad. I'm with you, too," James added.

"She did murder someone though. That person did have a family, maybe friends. He also might not have been a good person, but he did nothing against the law. I do not feel happy Sarah is going to jail, but I believe I would not be content if she did not. What message does that leave?" Aldrich responded.

"That works for someone like you, who was born with a platinum spoon in your mouth. For the rest of us, the justice system doesn't really work that way. We can't rely on it to be impartial. Jason might very well get off on a technicality, but Sarah's stuck, even though we all know that Jason deserves to be in jail more than anybody else. You can rely on the justice system because it favors you. It doesn't favor us," Rita exploded. Aldrich opened his mouth to respond when he saw Rita's eyes blazing fire and decided against it. *Smart choice*, James thought.

James noticed Ash and Samantha still talking at the last table and decided he should go pop by. "Great talking to you guys. Good luck for everything and while it was nice meeting you, I really hope I don't see any of you again," he said.

"I agree. I feel like murder follows you guys around, which I would love to avoid," Hemant responded. James got up and walked over to Ash and Samantha's table.

"Hey guys, I know yesterday was hard. How are you guys feeling?" James asked.

"Honestly, kind of rough. Not having Sarah here after we went through so much the past week just feels *wrong*. I'm not sure how long it'll take to get over it. I'm also still not over Aron being killed purely to frame someone. So yeah, it's not great," Samantha said.

"I know what you mean, I'm feeling the loss of Sarah and Aron as well, and you actually knew them," James replied.

"It'll be hard to keep continuing as normal when we get back. For sure, though, we won't forget this experience," Ash said.

"I noticed you said *we* a lot. Have you two finally confessed your love and all? Whatever the phrasing is," James asked.

"We did, we were just talking about it. We'll take it slowly for now and see how it goes," Samantha said.

"Especially because of the high stakes environment from the past week, there's a chance that our 'love' isn't real and is just a byproduct of a high heart rate and excitement that we're misattributing to each other," Ash added.

"You're the psychiatrist. I'm sure you guys will do whatever works best for you," James replied.

The captain's voice came on the intercom. "Greetings everyone. We are finally back in San Francisco! After the excitement of the past week, I hope each of you have a safe trip back home and more importantly, a relaxing time. Thank you for cruising with us!"

Everyone immediately stood up and began collecting their

things and walking out. Samantha also began to collect her things and looked at James. "Well, guess we're here. Time to head on out. Thanks again James for helping me throughout the voyage and especially tell Quentin I appreciate him finding the murderers. In this trip, you guys and Ash were definitely the highlights."

"Yes, thank you both of you. While I would like to see you again, I really hope it can be under much more pleasant circumstances with no murder involved if possible," Ash said.

Together, both of them began to walk out of the hall. "Guys, I…" James began. *I shouldn't tell them about Sarah's love for Ash. It's not fair to them and it's not helping anyone.*

"Yeah?" Ash turned.

"Nothing, never mind. Good luck!" James called out.

Soon, it was just Quentin and James left in the hall. James walked over to Quentin. "Let's go. The cops can handle Jason and Sarah. You need to go home. It's been a long week," James said.

"You're right. I can't say I'll miss it," Quentin said and looked around the hall one last time and walked out with James.

Together, they walked out onto the pier and to their cars. "Well, looks like it's time to go," James said.

"It is."

"I wonder when the next time will be."

"You know our luck. Wherever we go, murder follows."

"Then, until next time," James said as they both stared wistfully at the ship. The ship looked peaceful. There were no signs of all the blood that had been shed in just the prior week.

They waved goodbye and began to head back home as the sun set behind them.

Printed in Great Britain
by Amazon

85683514R00084